To my mother and father.

George Radley

THE THERAPEUTIC CHARITY SHOP

AUSTIN MACAULEY PUBLISHERS™

LONDON • CAMBRIDGE • NEW YORK • SHARJAH

A CIP catalogue record for this title is available from the British Library.

ISBN 9781788780186 (Paperback)
ISBN 9781788780193 (Hardback)
ISBN 9781528955041 (ePub e-book)

www.austinmacauley.com

First Published (2019)
Austin Macauley Publishers Ltd
25 Canada Square
Canary Wharf
London
E14 5LQ

To all the volunteers and managers at my local RSPCA Charity Shop who inspired me to write this book.

Chapter 1

It was a cold, wet Saturday morning in April and I was on my way to work with a spring in my step. This might sound strange but I was looking forward to going to work… as an unpaid volunteer at a charity shop. I had been working at the local RSPCA Charity Shop for four months now and I was enjoying it very much. I found the job very rewarding and satisfying. I felt like I was doing a worthwhile job. Also there was a good group of people working there. It's surprising that charity shops get so much criticism. Some people say that there are too many of them. That may be true in some areas but they do provide a good service for low-income people. I was pleasantly surprised at the high quality of the goods, especially the women's clothes. Many are from Marks and Spencer's, Laura Ashley and Next. Charity shops are similar to antique shops and second-hand shops. They can contain some hidden gems.

When I reached the shop, I saw Belinda, the manager, serving a customer. I said Good morning to her as I quickly passed her on my way to the back of the shop to put my coat away. I was the first volunteer in. I put the latest 'Bar Chart Sales Figures' on the wall of the manager's office. Shortly after I started working at the shop, I asked Belinda if I coul work out the percentage 'Sales Figures' for Saturdays. Sh agreed. I come from a quality control background, where v work out figures similar to this, so I thought it might interesting for me to do this.

Top of the sales were 'Women's goods', which norm; finishes top most weeks. Then came the 'Men's go followed by 'Bric-à-brac' and 'Books' were in fourth pl Further down the chart were 'CDs and DVDs', 'Child

goods' and 'Jewellery'. This 'Bar Chart' is useful for both Belinda, and the assistant manager, Rita, to study. They could then take action to increase the sales of certain goods, such as sales or special deals.

When I went out to the shop, I spoke to Belinda. She was in her late 40s, had a medium-sized figure and short brown hair. She dressed smartly in a dark blue trouser suit. I liked Belinda. She was a strong-minded woman but fair. She was friendly with most of the customers but she could be firm with them if they tried to take advantage by asking for big price reductions.

"How are things today?"

"A bit slow so far, Greg. It must be the rain," said Belinda.

"Hopefully, the rain will stop soon and things will pick up," I replied.

I then took over working on the till while Belinda went in the back to sort some stock out to bring out into the shop.

The layout and presentation of the shop really impressed me. It was a relatively large shop, much bigger than the other charity shops in this town. At the front of the shop were the 'Women's clothes', our biggest sellers. They were set out on rails in colour formation. All the red tops were put on the same rail as were the white tops, blue tops and green tops. Also, in this section were jackets, trousers, shoes and handbags, which were also colour coded. This separation of the colours gave the clothes an artistic look. The high quality of the clothes gave the impression of a women's clothes boutique.

Halfway down the shop, there was a set of three steps leading up to, firstly, the small men's section and then all other sections, books, children's items, toys, DVDs and CDs, Bric-à-brac, old records, tapes and pictures. There was a wide range of products on sale.

When I'm not working on the till, I tend to look after the 'Book Section', bringing out new stock. Not long after starting, I noticed how untidy and messy this section was. The hardback books and paperback books were all mixed together and it looked a right mess. I then asked Belinda if I could separate the two types of books, like they are in most

bookshops. She said it was all right for me to do this and I spent two hours sorting it out. Belinda was pleased with my efforts, saying it looked much better. This should attract more customers to them and hopefully increase sales.

I looked around the shop, there were only two customers in and both were browsing. Charity shops have loyal, regular customers who you get to recognise. Many are very nice and you can build up a good working relationship with them. A lot tend to browse looking for bargains. At this particular shop, there are several good deals. There is the book offer of 'Buy One Get One Free'. This does encourage customers to buy books. Despite the popularity of Kindles, books are still very popular. Another good deal is the '99p Rail', which is situated outside the shop, which is there to entice customers into the shop. One more good deal is the half price offer for Bric-à-brac.

Suddenly, several customers came in at the same time. This often happened. There can be only a few people in there and then a lot come in together. One was a mother with a baby in a pushchair. As we have stairs leading up to the back of the shop, this can inconvenience them. Some automatically leave them at the bottom of the steps but others are not sure what to do. A lot of the time, I make a joke of it. One young mother was in this situation so I said, "You can leave your pushchair by the counter if you like. We don't charge for parking, especially if you buy something." This usually gets a laugh or a smile.

I have a good sense of humour, so I try to joke around with the customers, making witty remarks. One example of this involved a woman who wanted to try a dress that was displayed on a mannequin high up on a shelf. She asked me to get it down for her, which I did. Then I struggled to get the dress off. I said jokingly, "I don't normally have this much trouble getting women's dresses off."

Another funny incident occurred when I emptied the clothing bank and I found several fox fur stoles in there. At first I was disgusted that someone had put real fur in an RSPCA Charity Shop Clothing Bank but later I made a joke about it to Belinda. I told her that when I saw them, I said, "Fur fox sake!" She found it amusing. Another funny incident involving foxes occurred recently. A man rang the shop to ask us if we could help him with his problem. A female fox had moved into his garden to give birth to three cubs and they had virtually taken over his garden. I jokingly said, "Have you thought about charging the fox rent?" He laughed. He made this call thinking the shop was a rescue centre, not a charity shop.

The other day, I was in the shop putting some stock out and I heard a teenage girl ask her mom to buy the swear box we had on display. Her mom refused. I then went over to the woman to tell her, "You should have said, 'No, I effing don't want it.'" The woman laughed.

Nearly every Saturday, there is a funny incident. These humorous moments make the job more enjoyable.

A couple of regular customers walked into the shop. One was a cross dressing man who wears women's clothes. He was wearing a long skirt today. His wife accompanied him. She seemed relaxed about her husband. No one seemed to be bothered about things like this these days. They chatted to me about a few items in the glass cabinet by the till but they didn't buy anything.

Some of these regular customers are browsers and rarely buy anything. I think a few of them only buy certain goods, such as DVDs or records, and they visit the shop to see if there is any new stock.

Another customer who visited the shop quite often was Rashid, a large, friendly, Pakistani man. He was wearing a coat I sold him a few weeks earlier. I said, "Nice coat."

He replied, "Yes, very good. How are you?" He shook my hand.

"Fine, thanks. What are you looking for today?"

"Nothing in particular. I am only looking around."

He then had a good look around the shop. Ten minutes later, he returned with a black jacket in very good condition, costing £5.99. I said to him that this was a real bargain because it would cost him four times this amount to buy it new. It was almost new as well. Rashid was very pleased and left the shop smiling. Another satisfied customer.

A woman approached me to ask if there were any classic novels in the book section. I looked but couldn't find any so I suggested I look in the back storeroom. I asked Belinda to take over at the till while I went in the back.

The back storeroom contained stock of not only books but also pictures, large items like chairs and tables to sell at car boot sales and electrical goods waiting to be tested. The bookrack was reasonably tidy. The different categories of books had been separated by another volunteer, Adam, into paperback novels, hardback novels, biographies, autobiographies, animal books and history books. They had been put into boxes and labelled. Adam had done a good job. I looked in the boxes of hardback and paperback novels for any classic novels. Most were modern novels of authors such as James Patterson and Lee Child. Unfortunately, I only found two. One was *A Tale of Two Cities* by Charles Dickens and the second one was *Jane Eyre* by Charlotte Brontë. They were in reasonable condition so I took them out to the customer. She looked at them and said she would buy them. I put the PLU code (the shop's own code number to differentiate each item) on and the price and she took them to the till.

Belinda said she would take over the till for a while, so I said I would put more books out on the bookshelves in the shop. There were two bookcases. One contained the hardback and paperback books that were sold at £1.25 to £2.50. These were part of the 'Buy One Get One Free' book offer. They included novels, particularly modern novels, history books, wildlife books, autobiographies and biographies. There were several big gaps on the shelves so I needed to bring out at least twelve books, six hardbacks and six paperbacks.

The other bookcase contained the 20p books, which were much older and in slightly worse condition than the more expensive books. Some were over five years old and had a slightly yellow look. I thought I would need about ten books to fill the gaps in the four shelves.

After sorting through the various boxes with novels in, I chose all the books I needed. I then went into the main part of the front storeroom to put the shop's code and prices on the labels to put on the books.

Chapter 2

It was mid-afternoon in the shop and I was on my way to the small kitchen in the back to make some drinks. Belinda wanted a coffee, the two other volunteers, Grace and Sharon, didn't want any drinks as they had brought in cans or bottled water. I fixed myself a green tea.

After taking Belinda her drink out to her on the till, I went back in and had my drink. I started chatting to Grace and Sharon. Grace was a 27-year-old attractive, slim woman with striking red hair who had been working at the RSPCA Charity Shop for nearly two years. She was a big animal lover who particularly liked dogs. She was friendly, caring and had a good sense of humour. She was also feisty but had a big heart.

When I asked her if she liked the job, Grace replied, "I love it. There is always something going on here and there are lots of interesting items donated. You can find some real gems here."

"Is it better than your paid job?"

"Oh, definitely. The volunteers here are so nice and the managers are so supportive," Grace answered.

"Didn't you have problems with your boss?"

"Yes, Greg. My manager has been bullying me for the last few months."

"Sorry to hear it. Are you looking for another job?" I asked.

"Yes, I am. I would like to be an assistant manager at a charity shop or work at an animal rescue centre."

Grace then had a call on her mobile phone and went away to speak to someone.

I then spoke to the other volunteer, Sharon, a 35-year-old single mother. She was filling in for Shelley who was away, ill.

I said, "What about you, Sharon? What work do you do?"

"I haven't got a job at the moment, I left my last job over a dispute with my former boss."

"What was it about?"

"I was working at a care home but they weren't paying my wages. I complained to my boss but she kept promising me she would sort the problem out but she never did. I had to get my union involved to force her and the owners to pay me."

"That sounds bad. I have had a lot of problems at several companies as well."

"What sort of problems?"

"My last company was terrible. The bosses exploited the workers badly. They had a secret pay rise policy so most non-minimum wageworkers rarely received a pay rise, usually every five years. The favourites though would get one every year. In addition, nightshift workers didn't get a nightshift allowance and there were CCTV cameras everywhere spying on workers."

"The place sounds awful," said Sharon.

"There was a toxic atmosphere there. It encouraged greedy and selfish workers to become tell-tales. They would also creep around managers. These workers saw it as a way of getting promotion, pay raises and overtime. It was a minority of workers but they made it difficult for other workers because you couldn't trust them and you had to be careful what you said and did in front of them, in case they went running to the bosses."

"Were there no unions?"

"No, there weren't," I replied. "Most of the workers there were foreign, either Asian or Eastern European workers, so they didn't want to complain or cause problems."

"How long did you stay there?"

"About five years," I responded. "It might sound a long time but the work was interesting. I was an inspector there and

16

there was a lot of variety to the work. Also, there were some nice people there as well."

"What made you leave?"

"I was made redundant. I was quite relieved to go because so many people there got on my nerves. There was this one inspector, Dean, in my department who was one of the worst of the lot. He was always creeping around the bosses and making out how good he was and how much he did. He was given pay raises every year. Sometimes, he told the rest of us in the Inspection Department about it, but most of the time he kept quiet. The bosses were very clever.

"They would give him extra jobs to do, almost in exchange for these pay raises. One year, it was Induction Training for new workers. The year after that, it was Health and Safety."

"What a creep," said Sharon.

"He had to do all these extra jobs as well as his own job as an inspector. Consequently, he didn't do enough work in the department. Other workers had to do some of his work. Also, when people were on holiday, he didn't do much to help out. I usually had to do nearly everything to cover for others. In addition, he was so untidy, leaving a mess everywhere he worked."

"What did the others in your department think about him?"

"This is where he was clever," I said, "he was very cunning and devious. He put on this nice guy act with the two women in my department. One of these women, a Polish woman called Agniezka, used to say how nice he was. He acted differently with me. When we were in the CMM room measuring work, he wouldn't speak to me unless I spoke to him. He didn't like me because I was more experienced than him and I was more popular with the workers than he was. Dean was jealous of me."

"What was your manager like?" asked Sharon.

"He wasn't too good. He was too weak, as weak as a ten-watt light bulb," I stated. "My boss was also easily manipulated by Dean. In fact, Dean used to do virtually what he wanted."

"He sounds like an awkward worker."

"Yes, he was," I replied. "He was very ambitious for himself. That is all right up to a point but he went way over the top by telling tales about people, creeping around bosses and behaving selfishly. I remember once he went on holiday to Spain for two weeks. While he was away, our boss asked me and another female inspector, Sabine, into the CMM room to complain that Dean had been measuring some work but not telling him when the sizes went out. He also said that Dean was not measuring another part."

"Why did he tell you this instead of Dean?" interrupted Sharon.

"Exactly what I thought at the time," I said. "I bitterly regret not saying to my boss, why are you telling us this instead of Dean? I should then have complained about the favourable treatment that Dean was getting and saying to my boss why he allowed Dean to get away with so much. The thing with me is that I don't like to tell-tales and get people into trouble. Now, I wish I had."

"I know what you mean," said Sharon. "Where are you working now?"

"I'm doing some work for an agency. It's zero contract hours, I'm afraid, so I am not guaranteed work. This agency has got me some inspection work and also work as a machine operator. Some of this work is very boring, clock crawlingly slow."

"I think I know what you mean. I have a friend who has worked for an agency. She has had several bad jobs."

"The work I did as a machine operator was on the nightshift and I was only paid the minimum wage, not even a night shift allowance," I added.

"That sounds bad."

"It's not even the worst job I have done. I worked in a Chicken factory for two weeks."

"But you are a vegetarian, aren't you?" stated Sharon.

"Yes, but I was desperate for work at the time. Fortunately, I managed to get a better agency job soon after."

We finished our break. Sharon and Grace resumed their work. The procedure in the front storeroom was that donated bags that people had brought in were put in two stalls, one for Gift Aid donations and the other for non-Gift Aid donations. Then the volunteers would open the bags to sort through the items. If there were clothes, they would check that they were reasonable quality. If they were, the clothes would be hung up to be steamed later. If the clothes were of poor quality, they were put in a ragbag to be taken away. A man came to take these bags of rags every Monday. He paid about £2 per bag. This ragman also bought poor quality shoes and handbags. Other items like handbags, shoes, Bric-à-brac, DVDs or books, if all right, were set aside to have labels put on with the shop's code and price on.

I watched Grace steaming some dresses. She worked quickly and expertly, running the steamer up and down the dresses. The steaming removed the creases from the clothes so they looked better in the shop.

I thought about what Grace and Sharon had told me about their bad experiences at work and also mine. I saw how happy they both were working at the charity shop. It seemed as if it really was therapeutic to work in a charity shop.

Chapter 3

Not long after arriving at the shop, Belinda asked me to keep an eye on a large group of customers. There were eight of them all together, three men, three women and two children. Sometimes, the shop had problems with shoplifters so I was on 'Shoplifter Watch'.

I focused on the three men looking at the men's clothes. One of them was acting suspiciously. He took a pair of trousers off a hanger and looked at them for a while, trying them for length on his tall frame. Next, he picked up another pair of trousers. I remember Belinda telling me that shoplifters wait for an opportunity to steal items when we are serving customers on the till. They wait until the shop assistant is distracted and walk out with them. My plan was to watch them and then if they do look suspicious, go up to them and remind them that there is a changing room for them to try the clothes on. So I did this. As I had spoken to him, he knew I was watching him closely. He put the trousers back on the top of the trouser rail and moved down the shop towards the others whom he had come in with, in the women's section.

Belinda was watching them carefully behind the counter but when the man approached them, they all left together. We had seen them off. I then took the trousers left on top of the trouser rail to give to Belinda to put them behind the counter in case, one of them came back for the trousers. I had seen this done before with another man who had returned thirty minutes later.

Another tactic shoplifters used was to take three items of clothing into the changing room but only come out with two items to put back on the clothes rail, making out the clothes didn't fit them. They would have put the other item of clothes in their bag while in the changing room. They would have disposed with the hanger by hiding it behind a sign we have in the changing room. They could also have left the hanger on the clothes rail and just took the clothes into the changing room. Sometimes, this would be done unobserved if the manager or volunteers were serving customers.

I had also seen CDs without the 'CDs' inside. They had been removed by a customer and the empty cover was put back in the rack. I had noticed this shortly after starting at the shop when I was serving a customer and looked inside the cover to see if the correct CD was in the case. When I noticed a few empty, I had to check every one. The stolen ones were usually the most popular ones, such as Rihanna or Adele.

Sometimes, you can suspect customers of being potential thieves when they are not. I remember a few weeks ago when a man came in the shop pushing a supermarket trolley, the large ones used in big supermarkets. I watched him carefully to see what he was going to do. I thought he was going to put a lot of goods in there and rush out. In fact, he appeared to be one those people with a mental illness. He could only push it up to the bottom of the stairs. He left it there while having a look at something in the men's section and then came down the steps and left. It was very strange. No one uses a supermarket trolley in small charity shops. I mentioned it to Belinda but she didn't seem too surprised. She has probably seen far odder things than that in her time…

Also, you can be fooled by customers who look honest but are not. I remember a nice, friendly woman who came in with her boyfriend and was looking at a lot of the women's clothes. She was talking to me quite a bit. When she was about to take five items of clothing in to the changing room, Belinda stopped her and told her she could only take three items in. The woman then turned nasty and shouted out that she wasn't a thief and wouldn't steal them. She then walked out the shop. Belinda then told me she was a shoplifter and she always had to keep an eye on her when she was in the shop.

The methods used by manager's to counteract shoplifters were to put all the DVDs in boxes behind the counter, only putting the DVD cover on display; put all the expensive designer brand clothes behind the counter and put one of each pairs of women's and men's shoes behind the counter in containers, leaving either the left or right shoe out on display. This stopped shoplifters taking these products. It was a constant battle of wits between the shop workers and thieves.

Occasionally, a large item of furniture was donated. Recently, a woman called in the shop to ask us if we took armchairs. We said, "Yes." She stated that she had bought one for her mother but it was too low for her to get up. It was no use for her mother so the woman donated it to our shop. It had only been used for three days. The armchair was real leather, brown and very comfortable. It came with a pouffe. Belinda valued it at £170. Eventually, after three weeks, we sold it for £150. A customer must have haggled over the price to get a £20 reduction.

A vintage pram and cot, similar to the one in the film *Mary Poppins* was also donated but this proved to be hard to sell despite the price being reduced from £90 to £50. Finally, we had to sell it in a car boot sale.

Sometimes we would receive some great donations. A few weeks ago, someone donated several classic albums from the 1960s and 1970s. They included Rubber Soul, Revolver and The White Album by The Beatles. *Let It Bleed* by the rolling Stones and Led Zeppelin IV by Led Zeppelin. As they were in very good condition, Belinda gave them high prices and put them on display near the till. They soon attracted interest from customers and they were all sold within a week.

Most donations though, are smaller. These are mainly put in black bags or in other small bags and are brought into the shop by the donors. If there are very large numbers of items or house clearances these can be collected by Paul, Belinda's partner.

One of the young volunteers, Natalia, a 16-year-old Polish girl, was changing the clothes on the mannequins in the women's section. Most were high up on shelves so I helped her by taking them down for her. She then changed the dresses or tops on them. This was done a few times a week to freshen up the shop. This can bring out the artistic side in the volunteers because they have the freedom to choose the type and colour of the item.

Natalia was on a Duke of Edinburgh Award scheme, which has three levels of programme, bronze, silver and gold. She was on the Silver scheme at the time, which was for children aged 15 plus. Part of this involved volunteering at a shop for 12 months. Charity shops perform a very useful function in giving youngsters training and experience. They also give opportunities for people to take NVQ at the shops. Natalia worked for two hours on Saturday mornings. As she was 16, she was not allowed to work on the till but she did do other jobs, such as to put stock out in the shop, change the clothes on the mannequins and help out in the front storeroom.

After putting the last mannequins back up on the shelf, I spoke to Natalia. "How are you finding working at the shop?"

"I like it. There are so many nice people working here," said Natalia.

"Are you planning to work in retail when you finish your Duke of Edinburgh Award?"

"Yes. I would like to work in a clothes shop. I love fashion and clothes so that would be my ideal job."

Suddenly, I heard a loud scream coming from the back of the shop. I rushed into the back to find Shelley, a 22-year-old volunteer, in an excited state.

"What's going on?" I said alarmed.

"I just saw this huge spider by the lockers. It was enormous," said Shelley.

"What did you do?"

Then, Grace interrupted, "It was a fake one because it didn't move. I stepped on it but there was no blood," stated Grace.

I then realised it was my joke spider that I had in my bag. It must have fallen out. I decided to admit it was mine.

"I am afraid it was my joke spider. It must have fallen out of my bag by mistake. I didn't mean to leave it there or frighten you."

"Oh, Greg!" they both groaned. "You fool."

"I'm not normally afraid of spiders but it was very big and quite realistic," said Shelley.

"I'm sorry about that. What do you normally do if you find spiders at home, Shelley?"

"I usually kill them."

"You don't have to. I try to get rid of them by not killing them. I find a newspaper or magazine and a bowl or deep container. Then I slide the newspaper or magazine under the spider, scoop it up and drop it into the bowl. Finally, I take it outside and put it in the garden."

"That's a good method of getting rid of them," said Grace.

"I don't like to kill anything if I can help it. Spiders don't mean us any harm. They are mainly male spiders looking for females. Only a few are dangerous, like the black widow spider."

"You're a vegetarian, aren't you, Greg?" said Shelley.

"Yes, I am. I don't believe in killing insects or animals. They are all living creatures and they have a right to live. The only exception would be if they were dangerous and threatened someone."

"That's a good philosophy but I don't think I could become a vegetarian," said Shelley.

"Nor me," said Grace.

"I thought that there would be more vegetarians working here as it's an RSPCA Charity Shop but it's not the case. I am the only one that I know about."

"Most of the people working here are animal lovers but I don't think we could take that next step and give up meat," stated Grace.

She went on, "I don't eat meat much, mainly on Sundays when I have a Sunday roast."

"It sounds like you are a flexitarian then, Grace. You don't eat meat for most of the week but you still have it a few times a week. More and more people are becoming like this," I stated.

"I'm a bit like that as well," said Shelley. "I've cut down on eating meat a lot for health reasons mainly, especially after that horse meat scandal three or four years ago," added Shelley.

"Oh, yes, I remember that. A lot of frozen meat products had horse meat in them," said Grace.

"Lots of the big supermarkets were caught up in the scandal. I don't entirely trust a lot of these food companies to produce healthy ready meals. That's why I have cut down on eating meat," stated Shelley.

"I can understand it. So people are reducing their meat intake for health and also for ethical reasons," I said.

"How many vegetarians are there in Britain now, Greg?" asked Grace.

"About four million but the figure is increasing every year. There's also about half a million vegans," I answered.

"Could you become a vegan, Greg?" asked Grace.

"No, I don't think I could. I would miss eating dairy products, such as cheese, chocolate, yoghurts and eggs. Also, I don't think that becoming a vegan is as environmentally sound as being a vegetarian."

"Why's that?" asked Grace.

"I read a report that said the vegan diet only ranked fifth out of ten diets in its ability to feed large numbers of people. The researchers said that if livestock was got rid of, farmers wouldn't be able to use as much land as was thought for growing crops as some of it's not suitable for growing food crops. Therefore, if everyone turned vegan lots of land would go to waste. It was found that a vegetarian diet was the best option and made best use of land."

"That's interesting because you would have thought that a vegan diet would be more environmentally good. I don't feel quite so bad now," stated Grace.

"I feel the same as well," added Shelley.

"I suppose, you don't have to be a vegetarian or a vegan to work here. I don't make much of a fuss about me not eating meat. I am fairly tolerant about other people eating meat," I said.

"So you are not like Morrissey and speak out a lot about the subject," said Grace.

I laughed. "No, I don't go that far. I respect Morrissey's views but I leave other people to make up their own minds. I don't think meat is murder like Morrissey."

"Does he think like that?" said Grace.

"Oh, yes. Morrissey had that famous album, *Meat Is Murder*, which he did while he was with 'The Smiths' before he went solo. He is a big advocate of animal rights. I am a big fan of The Smiths. They made some great music."

"That's a great name for a record," said Grace.

"You should check it out on YouTube. They are from before your time but their music still sounds great today. Many young people know about Morrissey but not about his time with 'The Smiths'."

"What songs should I listen to first?" said Grace.

"I would start with *Please, Please, Please Let Me Get What I Want*, *This Charming Man*, *Meat Is Murder*, *There is a Light That Never Goes Out* and *This Night Has Opened My Eyes*."

"OK. I will give them a try. I like pop and rock music so I should like them."

Chapter 4

It was the day I had been dreading. I was moving out of my house. I had lived there ever since the sad death of my mom twelve years ago so it had a sentimental value as I associated it with my mom. I also liked the house. It was a modest two-bedroomed, terraced house in a cul-de-sac near the town centre.

I looked in every room of the house to say my farewells to it, remembering many of the good times I had here. Eventually, I collected the last of my bags and reluctantly left, locking the door behind me.

I had to sell the house after my redundancy last October. I hadn't been able to get another full-time job, only agency work, which was often only three- or four-days' work at minimum wage. I struggled to pay the mortgage and the other bills. It got too much for me so I had to sell it.

I got a reasonable price for it but as the mortgage was big and I had to pay the estate agents, my solicitor's fees and also my brother and sister, who had both lent me money to help me out, there wasn't as much money as I would have liked left, probably just enough to buy a small flat.

I was lucky that I found another place just down the road for a reasonable rent. It was a house share with the landlady's son, Philip. He was 23 years old and one of these young people who stayed in his room a lot on his computer, going on social media, watching films online and speaking to his girlfriend on Skype. I had most of the house to myself, including the front room. I had brought a lot of my favourite pictures, prints of Turner, Van Gogh and Whistler and the front room looked really homely.

Philip was a large, easy-going man who was a bit lazy but not too irritating. He kept out of my way most of the time and only really talked to me when he saw me in the kitchen or when he wanted to tell me something.

Before I moved out of my old house, I had sorted a lot of my possessions out and decided which to take to my new place, which to donate to my RSPCA Charity Shop and which of the large furniture to donate to the British Heart Foundation to help low income people.

I had taken a lot of bags of my items to my charity shop on Saturdays when I worked there. It made sense to take a few bags each week before I moved out so I wouldn't have to take them in all at once.

I had donated several of my old pictures, including prints of Turner and Van Gogh pictures. As I only really have two rooms to put them up, my bedroom and the front room, I had a lot left so I gave them to the shop. Some of these pictures sold within a couple of weeks.

I also donated lots of books, CDs, DVDs, ornaments and clothes. I think it's not a bad thing to move house every so often because it enables you to sort through your possessions and have a good clear out.

I took in the last two bags of donations to the shop. Belinda was in and she said, "More donations."

"Yes. These are the last few items."

"The shop has done well out of you. What are they?" said Belinda.

"Some ornaments and a few more pictures. I'm having to downsize. I haven't got as many rooms to put my things in now. I'll fill a Gift Aid form in for them."

"It must be bad for you to leave your own house."

"Yes, it has been. I lived there for over ten years and it was my mom's old house."

"It must have had a lot of sentimental value for you then."

"It wasn't the house I was brought up in. It was the house my mom bought when she re-married. Although, I do have some very good memories of my many visits to my mom."

"I see. What is your new place like?"

"It's all right. The rent is £80 per week, including council tax, water rates, gas, electricity and the internet."

"That sounds like a good deal. Where is it?"

"It's in the same road. It was a bit strange just moving 50 metres down the road. I hired a removal van to move my things because I had several big items like my double bed, two armchairs and a fridge. I knew I would have problems getting the big bed down the stairs and the armchairs out of the front door."

"Did you have many problems then?" said Belinda.

"Yes. They had to put the bed out of the window and they took the front door off to get the armchairs out. In my new place, it wasn't so bad. They just had to take the stairs door off to get my bed up. It would have been more difficult if these removal men were not experienced."

"I understand. You didn't want any problems. Have you managed to fit all of your things in?"

"Yes. The advantage I had moving so close to my old house was that I could take small items to my new place a few days before moving in. I was able to take things like pictures, my computer, CDs, DVDs and books. This saved a lot of time on the day of the move."

"That was a good idea. I have moved a few times and it was very stressful. Was it stressful for you?"

"It was stressful on the day of the move but it was also stressful a couple of weeks before because I had to clear out everything from the back cupboard and shed by a certain time. There was so much stuff in both these places, some of it stuff that had been there for many years going back to when my mom lived there. I should have dealt with a lot of this years ago. Also, in the shed, there were a lot of old tools, paint tins and paint brushes there, which were my stepfather's."

"It sounds like you had a lot of things to sort out. What did you do with all the stuff from the shed?"

"I had to throw most of the paint and paintbrushes away. I kept some of the tools which were in reasonable condition. A lot were rusty. I paid a friend to take away the rubbish."

"Thankfully, you have got it all finished now. Did you find it strange to see most of your donated items on sale here?" said Belinda.

"A little bit. At least other people can make use of the things I don't want or don't have room for. It's a good way of recycling things," I answered.

Chapter 5

It was early July and the weather was very hot, about 30°C. Despite this good weather, the customers were staying away. The shop tried to attract more female customers by having a sale of dresses for half price. It was proving to be reasonably successful with sales going up. However, the shop had gone quiet. No one had come in for half an hour.

I began to chat to Belinda.

"How many years have you worked at this RSPCA shop, Belinda?"

"Nearly five years. I used to run another shop over in Whiteheath."

"Oh, yes, I know it. I have been in it a few times when I have been working over that way. It's not as good as this shop though. This shop's layout and goods, particularly women's clothes are better."

"Thanks. I agree but they do make more money."

"Why's that?" I said.

"It's because that shop is near the market and it benefits from that. It's in a better location than this shop."

"I see."

"Another reason could be because this town, Marwood, has more charity shops than Whiteheath. This town has about seven charity shops, whereas Whiteheath has about five," added Belinda.

"So the customers are spread over less shops over there."

"Yes, that's right. I am still trying to find ways to increase our sales," replied Belinda. We both watched as the first customer for a long while came in and started browsing. "How are you finding working here, Greg?" said Belinda.

"I like it a lot. There are a lot of good quality goods, the volunteers are nice and the managers are good. They are fair, appreciate you and don't take advantage of you like many of the old bosses I have encountered in factories…"

"I like the last bit," said Belinda, laughing.

"You do get a lot of job satisfaction working here, knowing that you are helping to raise money for animals and provide good quality items at low prices for low income people."

"I feel the same. Even though I am paid for doing this job, I get more job satisfaction from this job than I have from other jobs I have done," stated Belinda.

"I have read recently that working for a charity shop does make you feel better, both physically and mentally."

"I read about that too. You are a vegetarian, aren't you?" said Belinda.

"Yes. So this charity shop is probably my natural place of work. I have always been an animal lover. Another thing I like about charity shops is that they recycle so many things," I added.

"Yes, we recycle clothes, shoes and handbags which are not good enough to sell in the shop. Also, we recycle jewellery, old gold, coins, mobile phones and printer cartridges. A lot of things really. The shop is like a mini recycling centre! It stops a lot of things being sent to landfill."

"The only problem with this job is that I don't get paid as a volunteer. Can you do something about this?" I jokingly said.

"I only wish I could," said Belinda, laughing. "But it's out of my control."

"If you could, I would work here six days a week."

Just then several customers came into the shop so Belinda asked me to continue sorting through all the pictures in the back. I agreed and went away.

I had started going through these pictures in the back storeroom last Saturday so I carried on. There must have been over two hundred pictures of varying quality. There were prints of Constable, Monet and Van Gogh. The rest were pleasant pictures of the countryside, animals and boats. There were numerous religious pictures of Jesus and Pope John Paul, probably donated by Catholics.

I have always liked art so it was quite interesting to sort through these pictures. I separated them into piles—the larger, good quality ones in one pile, the smaller ones in another pile and the religious ones into another pile. There were also damaged pictures which I put on a pallet to throw away.

I then took out three of the best large pictures, one of which was a Monet print, put on the shops code and the price on the picture and then put them out on display in the shop. There were already about six large pictures out there so I made room for another three. By the time I had finished moving them around, it looked good. These pictures made this section look very pleasing on the eye, like a mini art gallery. I recognised several of these pictures because I had donated some of them months before, including a Turner print and two pictures of scenes from London which I had bought when I visited London many years ago.

Next, I sorted out twelve small pictures to put out in boxes on the picture section. There were already three boxes out there with pictures marked up as £1 each but they were selling fast so I topped them up.

While I was doing this, a customer asked me if there were any more pictures of boats. She had two in her hand but wanted more. She explained that she was fascinated by them. I said I would have another look in the back because I was sorting through them. I quickly went in the back and looked through another pile of pictures and sure enough, found another two prints of boats. I hurriedly took them outside to show them to the customer. She took a look at them and looked pleased with them. So she bought all four pictures. I was also pleased to be of help to her because it makes my job more rewarding when I can personally provide a customer with the products that they are looking for.

This often happens with a customer when there isn't the item they are looking for in the shop and volunteers and managers have to go in the back to find them the item they want.

Sometimes we have a disabled customer in who needs help. This happened a few weeks ago when I was working on the till. An elderly man came in on a mobility scooter, who was looking to buy some DVDs. As the DVD section is at the back of the shop up three steps, he couldn't get to them so I offered to bring some out to him. Firstly, I asked him what type of DVDs he liked, he replied westerns and war films. Then I searched the DVD section and brought out about a dozen films for him to look at. He chose two war films, *The Dam Busters* and *The Wooden Horse* and two westerns *Shane* and *True Grit*. He seemed very pleased and thanked me. I was also pleased to have helped him.

Belinda then called me over to ask me to take all the electrical goods we had in the back storeroom up to the top storeroom for testing, to see if they were safe to sell. It would be a big job.

There must have been over one hundred electrical items, such as radio cassette players, DVD players, CD players, record players, fans, microwaves and even a Christmas tree. It took me nearly two hours to take them all up the stairs, a large flight of about thirty steps. It was a worthwhile job as the back storeroom looked tidier. John, the electrician who would be testing these goods, was due in the shop the following week so it made sense for them all to be in one place for him to check them.

This shop had mainly women workers so this physically hard job was more suited to a man. As there were only two men working here, Adam and me, it was between me and him. Adam was overweight and probably not fit enough so I was asked to do the job. I didn't mind doing it. It was good exercise.

Chapter 6

Belinda was on a week's holiday so Rita, the assistant manager, was in charge of the shop. Belinda had gone down to Devon to spend a relaxing time there for her August holiday.

Rita was a little older than Belinda, probably in her late 50s. She was quite slim, average height and had nice blue eyes. Rita had been working there for nearly ten years, much longer than Belinda and she knew nearly all the customers. She had told me that she liked the job of assistant manager and preferred working part time, about three days a week, as well as filling in for Belinda when she was on holiday. Like Belinda, Rita was very popular with the volunteers. Both these managers treated the volunteers with respect and always thanked them for the work they did.

I thought back to some of the managers I had worked for, as an inspector. Some were all right and fair. My first manager, Tim, who had employed me in my first inspection job, had been good to me. I had a problem with another inspector, Diane, at the company, who had taken a dislike to me. She had told tales about me to Tim, deliberately stirring things up. I had got into many arguments with her and the atmosphere in the department was toxic. He moved me from my job as a patrol inspector to another part of the factory to become a final inspector, helping out a nice, friendly Final Inspector, Bill, who needed some help.

This solved the problem between Diane and me. I enjoyed the challenge of doing a different job and of working with Bill. I also had the satisfaction of seeing Diane get the sack a few months later. Diane started having a lot of time off and was sacked. She was a nasty, arrogant, tell-tale and bully.

Hardly anyone liked her so she wasn't missed. In contrast, Neil, the boss I mentioned to Sharon, wasn't that good. He was very weak and allowed another inspector in my department, Dean, to creep around the bosses and get pay rises every year while other inspectors, including me, could only get a pay rise every four or five years. Dean often went over Neil's head to get these pay rises and as a result thought he could do what he wanted.

I didn't get on too well with Dean so when there was a re-organisation of the department, I was made redundant. I didn't mind too much because I couldn't stand working with Dean. Also, the company wasn't fair to workers. It exploited most of the workers there. I had worked there for over five years but I was glad to leave.

I did have a terrible experience with one of my old quality managers, Gary. He was only in his late 40s, about 47-years-old, I think, when he had a heart attack at work and died in the Quality Office. Unfortunately, I wasn't in the office at the time and I found him too late when he had gone blue. When I saw him, I rushed to get someone who could do first aid. I found someone from the tool room, Brian, who gave Gary mouth-to-mouth resuscitation. Sadly, it was too late. Gary had a wife and three children so it was a big shock to them. I remember Gary telling me that he had filled in for a player, who was absent, for his son's football team. He played for the whole of the game and it took a lot out of him. Since then, he had felt bad. This over-exertion and the fact he was a heavy smoker sadly caused his early death.

So I have had some bad experiences with managers and also workers in my time so it made me appreciate Belinda and Rita.

Rita asked me to work on the till while she did some work in the front storeroom. I took over and worked there for a while. It was fairly quiet. These quiet periods never lasted long because customers would then come in clusters.

Despite the occasional quite period, a lot happened at this charity shop. It was hardly ever boring. It reminded me of most of the companies I had worked at as an inspector in the past. There were so many quirky and eccentric characters who came into the shop, the volunteers were interesting and every day was different.

A man came to the counter to buy a pair of trousers. I put it through the till and charged him £4.99. He offered me a £10 note and when I was about to take it from him, he pulled it away. I was a bit surprised at this. When he offered the money again, I reached for it and once more he pulled it away. All through this, he had a straight face but now he laughed and said in a joking way that he would complain about me not wanting to take his money. I laughed with him.

This man was a good example of an eccentric, one of the many that visited this shop. It was a good job I liked these types of people, I thought to myself as he walked out the shop. I did think about snatching the money from his hand and then laughing at him.

Another strange character that visited the shop was a middle-aged man who had taken a liking to Grace. When he called in, he would ask about her and try to persuade us to get her out so he could hug her. At first, we did this a few times but when he started doing this nearly every Saturday, Grace soon got tired of it and asked us not to let him know she was working in the back. I would pretend she was busy in the back storeroom doing a job.

An elderly woman came into the shop and stopped to talk to me. She mentioned the weather, the heavy traffic on the road and what she was looking to buy. We sometimes get people in the shop who are lonely and want to get out and about to talk to people. I didn't mind doing this because some of these customers are quite interesting to talk to. I also understood them as I had been through lonely times in my life in the past.

A woman and her young daughter came into the shop then to look at some women's clothes. After a few minutes, she approached me and asked me if her daughter could use our toilet as she was desperate. I wasn't supposed to do this because of health and safety reasons. Belinda had told me this many months ago. As Rita had gone upstairs to take some

37

bags up, I said she could, as long as she was quick. I also added jokingly to the girl's mother that she could go if she bought something. She laughed. I then showed the girl to the toilet, put the light on and left her. Fortunately, she was back out within a few minutes, before Rita had come down. The girl's mother thanked me.

A little later, this woman bought two T-shirts and a pair of shoes costing nearly £10 so it was worth it to help her daughter.

We also had our fair share of awkward customers. These were the type of people who asked you to get several T-shirts, tops and dresses down from the mannequins high on the shelves but would only look at them, change their minds and not buy them.

Some customers could be hard work as well. I helped a man find a suitable jumper recently but it must have taken him twenty minutes to decide which one to buy. I found him three in his size but he was indecisive and couldn't make his mind up. I left him to it and did another job. Eventually, he made a choice. As he was elderly, I had to be patient with him. It worked out all right because he got his jumper and the shop got the sale.

In addition, there were some mean people who shopped here. Some wanted price reductions on items that weren't all that expensive. An example of a customer's meanness happened recently when a woman wanted to buy a toy for her daughter. The price was £1.50, which was quite cheap. However, she asked me if I could reduce it to £1. I said we couldn't cut the price on goods as cheap as this. I explained that we do negotiate, on rare occasions, prices on more expensive products but not on items that cheap. She reluctantly bought it. Afterwards, Rita told me that this woman was the meanest customer we had in the shop. She was always trying to get reductions on goods even if they were fairly cheap.

Another mean customer was a man who bought a shirt for 99p but brought it back shortly afterwards. He wanted a refund. I explained to him that we didn't do refunds but asked customers to buy something else for the same price. I also told him that the reason why the shirt was so cheap was that there was a minor fault on it.

I know many of our customers are in low-paid jobs, unemployed or on disability allowance but some people try to take advantage of us.

Despite these small numbers of awkward and mean customers, most of the customers were friendly, caring and pleasant. Many made a point of visiting our charity shop because it raised money for an animal charity rather than for another type of charity. This showed their caring side.

Just then, one of my favourite female customers came into the shop. She was a tall, slim, Asian woman with dark hair, brown eyes and a very pretty face. She was probably in her early 30s. She visited the shop regularly and I always tried to talk to her. Her name was Raj.

"Hi, Raj, how are you?"

"Not too bad, thanks."

"What are you looking for today?"

"I am looking for a few more T-shirts now that the weather is hotter."

"If you need any help, let me know."

"All right. Thanks."

Raj was one of the many women in their 20s and 30s who visited the shop. There doesn't seem to be a stigma attached to buying clothes from charity shops anymore. In fact, charity shops are becoming more popular and cooler with young women. There are so many different and unusual styles of clothes sold at these places that women can find something distinctive to wear that they wouldn't at most other clothes shops. Also, since the banking crisis, many people are looking for more bargains in order to save money and you can get plenty of them at charity shops.

Rita took over at the till while I went in the kitchen to make Rita and myself some tea, black tea for Rita and green tea for me. I also made Sharon, who was filling in for Shelley again, a cup of green tea. Grace had brought her own drink in.

When I went back out to give Rita her tea, I chatted to her for a while. Rita had brought in her daughter's Jack Russell dog as her daughter had gone on holiday. He was called Jack and he was a friendly, loveable dog. He attracted a lot of attention from our customers, particularly children. I joked with our customers that we would accept a price for him if the offer was large enough, say £300. Rita took it all good-naturedly.

I said, "How are the sales today?"

After checking, she said, "£250, which is good. There is another half an hour left so we could do quite well."

"Not a bad day," I said.

Usually, if the shop took between £200 and £250 then that was a good day.

Chapter 7

I reached the gates of Dudley Zoo just after 10 a.m. Most of the other volunteers at the shop were waiting outside. We had arranged the day out only last week. The weather had been very hot in the last two weeks and some of us had been talking about going on a day out together on a Sunday. We were all animal lovers so we agreed to visit Dudley Zoo. I had heard there were some new attractions so I was looking forward to visiting it again.

Not everyone could make it. Belinda had arranged a day out with her friend and couldn't cancel it and Rita had to visit her elderly mother. However, Grace, Shelley, Sharon, Adam and I could make the day out.

Adam was the last one to arrive. We then went to the entrance to pay the fee of £14.50. This included visiting the zoo and the castle, which was quite good value. After getting our zoo guides, we decided to follow the guide and look at the animals in order. If there were some animals we didn't like much, we could move on quickly.

I asked everyone if they had seen the new Lorikeet Lookout feature, about colourful parakeet birds. Only Grace had seen them.

"It's very good. The birds are like parrots with very colourful feathers, mainly greens and yellows," said Grace.

"I heard you can feed them," said Sharon.

"Yes, you can. You can get a small bowl of nectar and put it on your hand. The birds will fly over to it and eat from it," added Grace.

"I bet they are popular with children," I said.

"Oh, yes, children love them. The birds sometimes land on your head," said Grace.

"I'm looking forward to seeing them," said Sharon.

We then started to walk slowly around the zoo. We firstly looked at the vibrant flamingos, the excitable spider monkeys, baboons and the Asian black bear, stopping to read the information boards informing the public all about the animals. Many were endangered species.

The two snow leopards were beautiful and we spent a bit longer looking at these lovely animals. They are very rare in the wild and are found mainly in the Himalayas.

Sharon was getting very excited at this point because her favourite animal at the zoo was coming up next, the Sumatran tiger.

"Tell us about them, Sharon," I said.

"They are of a beautiful colour with their orange and black stripes but not as big as the Indian tiger. Also, they are critically endangered, only 300-400 are left in the wild. There is a very good viewing area to see them, two large glass panels. Sometimes, they come right the way down to these panels and then you can get a great view of them," said Sharon.

"That sounds a bit scary," stated Sharon.

"It's quite safe. The glass is reinforced," replied Sharon.

I interrupted by saying, "There is some advice, at the back of this zoo guide, about what to do if an animal escapes."

"What's that?" said Grace.

"Run!" I said jokingly.

"Let's hope that doesn't happen," said Shelley, a little shakily.

"There was the recent tragedy of a tiger getting out of its enclosure and attacking and killing a zookeeper," I stated.

"Yes, I remember it. That was sad. Tigers are beautiful but very dangerous," said Adam.

We then arrived at the Sumatran tigers' enclosure. Sharon rushed over to it but was disappointed that the two tigers hadn't come down to the glass panel. We could just see them in the distance.

"Let's wait a while to see if they come down," said Sharon. "Okay. Let's give it ten minutes," I stated.

So we waited patiently for them to come closer. Just when we were about to move on, they came down.

"Wow!" said Sharon, "They are magnificent."

"I can see why you like them," said Shelley.

"The male's name is Joao and the female's name is Daseer."

We spent about five minutes admiring them and taking lots of pictures before the tigers moved to the back of the enclosure.

The next group of animals we looked at included the lynx, red pandas and giraffes.

We spent quite a lot of time watching the family of Rothschild's Giraffes. I have always quite liked them, their great height making them stand out from other animals.

"It must be awkward being so tall," stated Sharon.

"I'm not sure how they sleep," said Shelley.

"I saw a wildlife documentary about them. In captivity, they sleep lying down but in the wild they rarely sleep on the ground because of predators," said Grace.

"It would be interesting to see how they do lie down," said Sharon.

"In this wildlife film, it shows how they do it. They drop their front legs first and then their back legs afterwards," answered Grace.

"That sounds quite awkward. It's a shame for them," said Shelley. "They are such gentle animals."

"They are most of the time but in this documentary, two male giraffes were fighting over a female in order to mate. It was a ferocious fight with each one banging their heads against each other's bodies," said Grace.

A large family of six, including four very excited children then appeared so we moved on to look at the anteaters, the tortoises and the parrots. Then, we came to Lemur Wood, the woodland home to four species of lemurs.

"This is my favourite place in the zoo," I said.

"Why do you like it?" asked Grace.

"It's partly the lovely lemurs but I also like the wooded enclosure because it's big and stimulates the animals."

We then walked through the secure gate making sure we locked it. Inside, there were hundreds of trees and shrubs for the lemurs to climb.

We read the information board, just inside the enclosure. It said that there were four types of lemurs—ring tailed, black and white ruff, black lemurs and collared lemurs. In all, there were eighteen lemurs, all from Madagascar.

"There's one lemur here who is very mischievous. He's always trying to unlock the gate and he has been successful many times. They have had to change the type of lock to a more secure one," I stated.

"I can see how naughty they are," said Grace. "Did you see that lemur trying to take that man's bag?"

We spent the next half an hour wandering around the wood, watching the antics of the lemurs. Some were walking along the fence, some were in the trees and some were by a group of schoolchildren having their pictures taken with them.

"I can see why you like them," said Grace. "They are loveable creatures with big, beautiful eyes."

"Which are your favourite animals here, Grace?" I asked.

"I like a lot of the animals here but my favourite ones are the meerkats. They are so funny."

"They are coming up fairly soon," said Shelley, looking at the zoo guide.

"What time are we having lunch?" said Adam, hungrily.

"It's nearly one 1 p.m. What about having it now?" I said.

"Yes. That should be all right. What about having it near the castle?" stated Sharon.

We all agreed and we went to the castle. Dudley Castle was built in the 12th century but it became a ruin following the English Civil War and a bad fire in the 18th century. It's a Grade 1 listed building now. Perhaps the best feature of the castle is the keep. In 1937, the Earl of Dudley opened the zoo and brought animals from all over the world to fill it, in the grounds of the castle.

We had all brought food and drinks to cut down on the amount we spent. Sharon and Shelley sat together on one bench while Grace, Adam and I sat on another bench.

"Are you both enjoying the day?" I asked.

"Yes, it's been very good," said Adam.

"It's been great so far," added Grace. "We have still got to see the lions, Reptile World, the meerkats and Lorikeet Lookout so there are plenty of animals left to look forward to," stated Grace, enthusiastically.

"What are both of your impressions of the zoo?" I asked.

"I have been to a few other zoos but I still think it's one of the best zoos in the country and it does have many endangered species," said Grace.

"What about you Adam?" I inquired.

"I agree with Grace. I think what makes this zoo so special for me is that it is in the grounds of Dudley Castle. It's a very good setting. I don't know of any other zoos like this," stated Adam.

"I'm a fan of the zoo as well. But do you both approve of zoos?" I said.

"It's a difficult question to answer. I like to see animals living in the wild but so many animals are endangered so there is almost a need for zoos these days," added Grace.

"Also, we are the main cause of the decline in so many animals' numbers. We hunt them and destroy their habitats," added Adam.

"I have some friends who are animal rightists and they don't believe in keeping wild animals in captivity at all, for any reason. They reckon if some animals become extinct so be it," I stated.

"That's a bit harsh. I don't agree with that view," said Grace.

"Nor me," added Adam.

"I don't either. I have had many disagreements with them but I respect their views," I stated.

"If zoos were made illegal a lot of animals would be extinct by the end of the century. There are too many greedy, selfish people around who don't respect animals and who make money from them and kill them for pleasure," declared Adam.

"It's disgusting that poachers kill beautiful animals like elephants for their ivory and also rhinos for their horns," said Grace.

Just then Sharon and Shelley came over to our bench. They had eaten their lunch. Sharon asked us if we all wanted to climb up to the top of the castle to look at the views. We all agreed so we set off towards the castle. We spent half an hour looking at the magnificent views of Dudley and the surrounding countryside. There was a nice cool breeze blowing to cool us down after the heat of the morning when it was 30 degrees.

Later, we resumed our tour of the zoo. The lions were the first animal we looked at. They were typically sleeping and not doing much so we moved on to see the orangutans and the reindeer until we came to the Reptile World.

"This is my favourite place in the zoo," stated Adam. "I am a big fan of snakes."

So we entered the Reptile World enclosure. Inside were several different kinds of snakes, including boas, pythons and corn snakes. Also, there were iguanas, bearded dragons, geckos, lizards, turtles and tortoises. As we wandered around looking at these colourful reptiles, I asked Adam about the glass enclosures.

"Do you think that these glass enclosures are big enough?"

"No, I think they should be bigger. Many of these snakes are long in length and should have more space," replied Adam.

"There does seem to be quite a lot of stimulating items in some of the turtle's enclosure, such as the pool, waterfall and tropical foliage," said Grace.

"Yes, in some of the enclosures, there is a lot to stimulate the animals but I would like the snakes' enclosures to be larger," added Adam.

We spent around half an hour looking around Reptile World, marvelling at the snakes and the bearded dragon.

"What's next?" said Shelley.

"It's the meerkats," said Sharon, looking at the guide.

Grace looked pleased and hurried over to see them. Most were lying on their backs basking in the sun. One was standing on tiptoe looking around for predators, the lookout. A couple of the younger ones were play-fighting and running around. There was a big crowd of people watching them, the biggest group of people we had seen so far.

After about forty-five minutes, we dragged Grace away, saying that the penguins were nearby. I took several photos of Grace and the meerkats to put in the newsletter.

The penguins were Humboldt penguins and they were loveable animals as well. They looked funny when they walked on land but they were expert swimmers in the pool. There was a colony of seventy penguins at the zoo, which is quite large.

Before reaching the Lorikeet Lookout, we had a look at the two red squirrels. One of the squirrels was behaving a bit bizarrely, rocking from one foot to the next. He looked like he was stressed out and probably bored. It was a bit disturbing. We commented on it. It was the only time we had seen an animal either stressed out or bored.

The chimpanzees were next. They are always worth watching. Their enclosure had many swings and ropes for them to play on. We spent about half an hour watching them running around, swinging from the ropes and play-fighting.

Lastly, we went to the Lorikeet Lookout. We had to go in an enclosure which had several trees and bushes. Most of the parakeet birds were on the trees. Then, a family comprising of three children appeared with some bowls of nectar held out in their hands. Suddenly, the birds swooped down and landed on the children's hands, greedily lapping up the nectar. Another bird landed on one of the parent's head, which amused the children.

We then spent quite a lot of time looking at these colourful birds, watching them feed on the nectar and fly around in the trees. It was nearly 6 p.m. so we had to make our way home. Everyone had an enjoyable time. We then went our separate ways.

Chapter 8

It was late September and the weather was getting a little bit colder. Most Septembers, in recent years, have been much milder, with mainly dry and sunny days so the summers have been prolonged. It almost seems as if the summer has been put back a few months now, from August to October rather than from June to August as in previous years. Maybe, it was global warming.

At this time of year, the winter clothes were usually brought out. This included women's and men's clothes. Recently, a rich woman had donated half a dozen imitation fur coats of various colours. Belinda had given them high prices. This didn't deter any of the women. Almost immediately, female customers were looking at them, some trying them on. I sold two of these coats to two different women, one at £15 and the other at £25. Another woman wanted a reduction in the price by £3 or £4 but Belinda wouldn't agree. She told me that she was sure she could get a sale at the top prices without reducing them. Belinda was proved right because she sold two coats later on for the full value. It was her experience that made her so certain.

Men's wax jackets and heavy overcoats were also put out and these soon attracted interest from some men.

Later on, Belinda put what was left of the summer clothes, mostly women's, in black bags and piled them up for me to take upstairs to the top store room. While I was up there, Belinda had asked me to separate the bags of women's goods and men's goods for rotation.

These are items that haven't sold so they will be taken to other RSPCA shops. Then goods from other shops will be sent to our shop. Also some of these rotated goods would be going to the new RSPCA shop that was due to open in Birmingham soon.

Rita then appeared in the shop along with her granddaughter, Indiana, who was starting a Duke of Edinburgh award scheme for six months. She would be working for one hour each Saturday. She had replaced Natalia, the Polish girl who had left earlier in the month.

Indiana was 14 years old, about 5 foot 4 inches, slim with blonde hair. She seemed quite friendly. I spoke to her about the book section. I asked her if she was a book lover.

"Yes. I like books. I read all the time."

"Who are your favourite writers?"

"J.K. Rowling is my favourite."

"Ah. You're a Harry Potter fan then?"

"Yes, I can't get enough of them. Unfortunately, there are not many new ones now, only the illustrated ones. So, I re-read the old ones."

"We don't have many Harry Potter books donated. There were a couple last month."

"I think most people want to keep them after they read them," said Indiana.

She went away to put some new stock out of women's dresses in the women's department. I went to bring out more books as the shelves were looking empty.

Shelley hadn't turned up again. She normally came in at 2:00 p.m. and did the afternoon shift, working until the shop closed at 4:45 p.m. She has had a lot of Saturdays off since she started working here in March. Belinda had been fairly lenient with her, allowing her to come in when she wanted and letting her have lots of time off. Some of this time off was because her mom was ill but some people suspected that Shelley was taking advantage of this situation.

As volunteers of charity shops don't get paid, managers have to be quite accommodating about the hours they can do. Many volunteers fit their hours around their families or work commitments, doing maybe three or four hours each day. I work six hours on Saturdays because I work in the week. I have done a few other days in the week such as Fridays when

I was in between work. Grace does three hours on Saturday and Sharon usually works for three hours on Thursdays and Fridays.

The problem with Shelley though was that she didn't always ring up to let Belinda or Rita know she wouldn't be coming in. Then Belinda or Rita could get someone else in to cover for her. In recent months, Sharon has been filling in for Shelley when she hasn't turned up.

A little later, Belinda came to me and said that she had just rang Shelley to speak to her about all the time she has had off.

"I have just rung Shelley to tell her that I don't want her to come back here. I explained to her that I needed more reliable volunteers to work at my shop, people to turn up regularly."

"What did she say?"

"She said she was sorry she had so much time off but she has lost interest in working here.

"Also, she wants a Saturday job that pays. I said that was fair enough and I thanked her for working here for about six months."

"It's a shame about her. She's a nice girl."

"Yes. She's a nice girl and she worked hard when she was here but she was causing me lots of problems with staff. I want volunteers to come in regularly and let me know in advance, if possible, if they can't come in, I can then usually get other people to come in," said Belinda.

"I understand," I said. "If she was working at a company where she was paid, she would have been given written warnings or been given the sack."

"Yes. That's right. I have let her get away with too much in the last few months."

"Are you going to advertise for someone else?"

"Yes. I am going to put a notice up in the window to get someone else. In the meantime, I will ask Sharon to cover for her," added Belinda.

Just then a man brought in three bags of donated goods. This happened fairly regularly each day, the number of bags varying with each person. People were good enough to donate their old clothes, books and other items. The quality of the goods did vary. They could be high quality branded women's clothes from Marks and Spencer's, Laura Ashley and H&M. Many times these clothes wouldn't have been worn or maybe worn just once.

Of course, we received some bad stuff as well. Certain people see charity shops as a way of getting rid of their rubbish. One person donated an old duvet that was heavily stained. They should have thrown it away. We accepted the duvet and sold it to the ragman.

Another person donated two bags of carrier bags, the ones you have to pay 5p for now. This person must have had them in the house for years and had a clear out. I don't know what we were supposed to do with these carrier bags. We couldn't sell them. We put them to one side and gave some out free to customers who bought a lot of goods.

We have received lots of other strange donations in the time I have been here. Grace found a pair of pink, fluffy handcuffs. A label on them said, "Not suitable for children under 15." That was funny and odd. Another strange donation was a book about male nudes. I had a sneaky look inside and most of the pictures were quite graphic, full frontal nudity. Now if only…

I wondered if we should be selling it. It should have an x-certificate.

Other donations came into the shop through collections by Paul, Belinda's partner. If there were lots of bags or house clearances, he went to people's houses and brought them back to the shop. This was a useful service for elderly people who couldn't carry many bags or didn't have cars to take several bags to the shop.

Another way donations reached us was the clothing and shoe bank outside the shop. This was mainly for customers to put their donations in when the shop was shut. Some people, however, put bags of donations in there while the shop was open which meant that it could be full by the end of the week.

Therefore, we usually emptied it on Fridays, in time for the weekend.

I remember a few weeks ago when a woman put a very full bag into the clothing bank and got it stuck. Consequently, I had to take all the items of clothes out and put them into two large bags. It was so tight that it took me about ten minutes to get everything out of this bag into these other bags. The woman shouldn't have done this. As the shop was open, she should have brought it into the shop or at least put the items into two bags so it didn't get stuck. She caused me a lot of problems and I was cursing her.

The thing is, we didn't always know what was in these bags. It could be ordinary items, rubbish or treasure. I took all these bags into the front storeroom and put them in one of the two storage pens. I told Grace and Sharon that there were more bags for them to sort through. Grace mentioned to me that she had seen a really good T-shirt she liked. She showed me it. I told her it looked nice.

I had to smile at Grace's enthusiasm. She was very fashion-conscious and was always looking for a bargain. She must have bought dozens of items at the shop since I have been there.

Chapter 9

The new volunteer, Jack, was working behind the till when I arrived at the shop, at 10:30 a.m. Belinda introduced me to him when it became quiet. I don't always like to judge people until I have known them for a while so I reserved judgement on him at first.

Jack used to work at another charity shop down the road from us, Age UK, for a few years so he was used to how a charity shop operated. He was middle-aged, probably in his mid-50s, medium build and dressed quite casually in a T-shirt and corduroy trousers.

Belinda gave me a job in the back storeroom sorting books out. We had lots of books donated recently so I was asked to sort them out. Firstly, I separated the hardback books and the paperback books. Then, I sorted them into different categories, fiction, autobiographies, history books, cooking books and so on. I didn't mind doing this because I do have a love of books. I expected to work on the till later. Belinda looked through the bags of donations in the front storeroom.

After my break, I thought I would be asked to work on the till but Belinda told me to help Grace in the front storeroom. When Jack wanted a break, Belinda covered for him. He went out to buy a snack and also have a smoke outside. I spoke to Sharon about this. She seemed puzzled by it too. Ominously though, Sharon didn't like Jack. She said he seemed unfriendly. He didn't say much to her when she saw him. Mind you, he didn't say much to me when I saw him a few times.

When Grace came in at 2:00 p.m., she was surprised to find Jack working on the till. She took over from Sharon and sorted through the donated bags. I helped Grace in the front storeroom, opening bags of items that were not clothes such as books, DVDs, Bric-à-brac. I left the clothes to Grace, who was probably the best at judging whether clothes were good enough to sell or to put out as rags. I emptied the full bags of rags, the full bags of shoes and the rubbish bags when they were full. I was Grace's 'Assistant sorter & bag changer'.

Every so often, I took out into the shop some of these items that had been sorted and had been priced. I did try to make an effort to speak to Jack when it was quiet but he didn't answer too many of my questions. He only said he had worked down the road at Age UK for a couple of years but didn't say why he left. He appeared to be fairly secretive about many things.

At the end of the shift, Jack left before Grace and me but didn't say goodbye. As Grace and I were tidying up the front storeroom, Grace told me that she didn't like Jack at all. "There's something about him that I don't like," said Grace.

"What is it you don't like about him?" I inquired.

"He's selfish and unfriendly."

"I have to admit I don't find him that friendly as well. Maybe we should wait a while and give him a chance. It's his first day."

"OK. I will see what he is like next week," said Grace.

"What are you planning to do on Sunday?" I asked.

"Not much. I will have a rest at home, relaxing. I might do a few articles for the newsletter."

"OK. Thanks. Just send any articles and features over. You always do good quality pieces."

"What are you planning to do?" asked Grace.

"The same as you, just relaxing, reading, watching some television programmes I have taped and doing some more items for the shop's newsletter," I replied.

The following Saturday, Jack was on the till again. Belinda asked me to sort through more DVDs on display in the shop for scratches. I had done this a few weeks before. I got the feeling Belinda was just finding me work to do in order to see how good Jack was.

While doing this job, I heard Belinda ask Jack to put several books out on the 'Book Section'. He went to do this but returned to speak to Belinda again. Slightly irritated, Belinda showed him where to put these books. Apparently, Jack thought the books weren't in alphabetical order because he couldn't find the relevant places to put the new books. I heard Belinda tell him that the books were in order. I couldn't believe that Jack couldn't put some books in the right place in a bookshelf. It was so easy a child could do it. I wondered if he had dyslexia. I then realised that this was probably why Belinda kept putting him on the till because he was a bit limited in what he could do at the shop.

I got a bit more insight into Jack's character when I was rushing to finish off my job before lunch. I had piled up several DVD covers to go back on the shelves and had separated the scratched ones to be reduced in price to 50p. The shop had no customers and he was on the shop floor wandering around doing nothing when I called him over to ask him to help me finish off by putting the covers back on the shelf and also mark up the scratched ones to the lower price and put them out on the 'Bargain Table' in front of the shop. He helped me put the covers back on the shelves but he didn't want to do the second job. I wasn't too impressed by his unhelpfulness. I would have to do them myself, after my break.

After popping into a few shops and then calling home to have a quick meal, I returned to the shop at 2:00 p.m. I took the scratched DVDs into the front storeroom and then put the shops code and price on them, 50p. I then took about twelve of these DVDs out to put on the 'Bargain Table' in front of the shop. As I was taking them out, Jack called out to me to tell me not to put too many out as there wouldn't be enough room. I told him I would have a look. There was enough room after all so I put them out. I was puzzled by Jack's behaviour. Was he trying to be helpful or trying to be my boss? If it was the latter, I wouldn't stand for that.

During the next few Saturdays, relations between Jack and the rest of the volunteers deteriorated so much that we tried to avoid him as much as possible. He was selfish, unfriendly and arrogant, all the qualities you wouldn't have thought a charity shop volunteer would have. He just didn't seem to be the type of person to work in a charity shop. I don't know why he wanted to work in one at all.

Before Jack came, there was such a good atmosphere at the shop. Everyone got on well with each other. We all took turns to work on the till and do our fair share of the less glamorous jobs. I even thought of a nickname for him— 'Jovial Jack', which we all found amusing and was very appropriate for him as he hardly smiled, was so gruff and hardly ever seemed to be in a good mood.

I didn't blame Belinda too much in all this. Even though she was the only person who actually liked Jack. I think Jack acted differently in front of Belinda. He put on a nice guy act when she was around. He was very sly.

After about another month of 'Jovial Jack's' unfriendliness, I decided to have a Saturday off. I had a dentist appointment in the morning and I had to do some canvassing work that weekend. This involved delivering election cards to people's houses. I had two weeks to deliver them but I thought I could have a Saturday off from working at the shop. I could go to the dentist in the morning and deliver the poll cards in the afternoon.

I wouldn't have done this if it wasn't for 'Jovial Jack.' I could easily have gone to work at the shop after my dentist appointment and delivered the election cards on Saturday evening and Sunday. I thought, *Why should I be bothered?* Prior to this, I hadn't had a day off from working at the shop in nine months. I had always been like this with all the places I have worked at. In fact, I had worked at my last place for five years without having a single day off. That was a record I was proud of.

When I told Belinda about this, she was surprised, mainly because I hadn't had any time off before. I didn't tell her that I was fed up of Jack. I didn't want to rock the boat and cause problems.

The following Saturday, when I returned, Grace told me that things hadn't gone that well and that they had missed me. Jovial Jack's gruffness was starting to have an impact on the customers. A few complained about him.

In addition, Grace was due to have a minor operation on her arm that meant she would be away from the shop for two weeks. This would be in a month's time. She told me that she might have longer off as it wasn't too good working at the shop anymore. It seemed like no one on Saturday was too keen to work with Jack. It reached a point when I was seriously considering approaching Belinda about his bad attitude towards Grace, Sharon and me. Then something happened to change everything…

There had been a few problems with discrepancies on Saturday's, where the money in the till didn't tally with the figure on the till receipt. As Jovial Jack was the main worker on Saturdays, he was questioned by Belinda. He must have given her convincing reasons because he continued working there.

These incidents should have been a warning to Jack but the incident that got him into trouble was a donation. A man had donated £100 to the shop. Normally, we tell the manager or assistant manager to put the donation through the till. However, Jack didn't put this donation through the till himself or ask Belinda.

It seemed that Jack had pocketed this £100. He didn't realise that this man knew Belinda and had told her he would be donating this amount of money on that day.

When Belinda came to cash up later, she checked for this donation and didn't see it. She rang this man straight away and he confirmed he had called in earlier and given it to the middle-aged man on the till. Belinda then suspected that he had taken it.

Jack worked on a few more days in the week, including Mondays so Belinda confronted him about this missing money. At first, he denied any knowledge of it but when Belinda informed him that she knew the man, Jack finally admitted taking the money. He stated that he was short of money because he was out of work and needed to pay a bill. Belinda told him to go.

Belinda told me about this when I first went in on the next Saturday morning when I saw that Jack wasn't there. She instructed me to go back on the till. I was relieved that Jovial Jack had gone. For the six weeks he was there, the atmosphere at the shop was bad. I didn't let Belinda know how pleased I was, though.

Grace and Sharon were very pleased to find Jovial Jack gone.

"I wish I had known before so I could have bought some cakes to celebrate," said Grace.

"And me," stated Sharon, laughing.

"Thank goodness for that," I added.

"I thought we were lumbered with him for ages," stated Grace.

"We can get back to normal now," said Sharon.

"You know this charity shop has a habit of solving our problems. This is another example. It's truly a therapeutic charity shop," I said.

Chapter 10

It was mid-October and Halloween wasn't far away. Belinda and one of the volunteers had done this wonderful Halloween display. It looked so atmospheric and spooky. There were lots of cobwebs, spiders, facemasks and costumes. Other features included some DVDs of horror films, *Witchfinder General*, *An American Werewolf in London* and *The Village*, the first television series of *The X Files*, a CD of ACDC's *Highway to Hell* and a book about ghosts.

I congratulated Belinda on the display.

"How long did it take you?" I said.

"About two hours. Sharon helped me on Friday afternoon when it was a bit quiet."

"It's impressive." I like the way that you can do these displays in shops. I remember the Valentine's Day display was good as well.

Just then, a woman and her two children came into the shop and looked at the display. The two young children, aged about nine or ten, were very interested in the masks. I went over to them and jokingly said, "If you buy a mask, you can have a spider free. It will be a buy one get one free offer."

They laughed and carried on into the shop.

While Belinda went to work behind the till, I looked around the shop floor to see if any stock needed to be brought out. When I was checking on the CDs and tapes, Sadie, the new volunteer, came out and spoke to me. She was in her mid-twenties, mixed race with a pretty face and dark hair.

"How are you finding the job?"

"I like it a lot," said Sadie.

She asked me about the two Police tapes, 'Regatta de Blanc' and 'Ghost in the Machine', in the tape section.

"A man at work I like is a Police fan."

"They were a really good British group from the late 1970s to early 1980s. In fact, they were one of the best groups in the world in the early 1980s."

"Which of these two tapes is the best?" asked Sadie.

"I like them both," I answered. "*Regatta* has *Message in a Bottle*, and *Walking on the Moon*. Both of these are great pop/rock songs," I stated.

"While *Ghost in the Machine* has other great songs on like *Invisible Sun*, *Everything She Does Is Magic* and *Spirits in a Material World*," I added.

"Which one shall I buy?"

"Both. They are only £1 each and they are both worth having."

"OK," said Sadie, "I'll buy them both."

"You could leave both the tapes on your desk at work. Maybe the man you like might see them. Then you can impress him with your knowledge of the group."

"I might do that," replied Sadie as she walked away to the counter to buy the two tapes. Belinda charged Sadie half price so she only paid £1 for both tapes.

Later on, Belinda asked me to show Sadie how to operate the till. Belinda was pleased with how Sadie had settled in at the shop and wanted her to do more duties. The till at this charity shop was different to other shops where they scan the goods. At this shop you had to do things manually by, firstly, inputting the shops code and, then, the price. I showed Sadie several times how to operate the till and then I told her to watch me do it a few times. After half an hour, she seemed a bit more confident and was willing to give it a try. I watched her serve a few customers without too many problems but she wanted me to remain with her for a while so I stood next to her.

In between serving customers, I spoke to Sadie. She is a bubbly, talkative and likeable character, someone who could talk for a long time. In fact, I could hardly get a word in when she got talking.

I asked her about her job.

"What job do you do?"

"I work at the bank doing the administration work."

"Do you like it?"

"It's all right but I would like to do something else, possibly to do with languages as I have a degree in French."

"That's useful to be able to speak another language and should help you get another job!"

"I am looking for other jobs at the moment," replied Sadie.

I jokingly said, "Have you had any problems with your boss or other workers?"

"Yes. My former boss was bullying me and a few other workers. She was treating us unfairly. It went on for two months until we reported her and she was removed from the job and found other work at the company."

"That's incredible because Grace, Sharon, you and me have had problems with managers."

"So many people who work here have had problems at work. Do you like working at this charity shop?"

"Yes. It has a good atmosphere. What about you? How long have you worked here?"

"About nine months. I started in January."

"Do you like it here?" said Sadie.

"I do like it. I find it relaxing to work here. I was made redundant from my job last October and it took me many months to find regular work. I also lost my house earlier in the year."

"That sounds terrible," stated Sadie.

"It has been a tough time for me in the last year but working here has helped me get through it."

"I have heard that working at charity shops makes you feel better," said Sadie.

"I have as well. I think the survey is accurate. I have found working here has helped me deal with stress and has made me forget my problems."

"I know what you mean. I have only been here a few weeks and I have found it very relaxing to work here."

"Yes, it helps a lot if you have a good group of volunteers to work with. You can have interesting discussions with them and have a few laughs," I stated.

"You also get a good feeling when you help customers to find the right item," added Sadie.

"That's almost the 'perfect job', except for one thing."

"What's that?" said Sadie.

"We don't get paid," I said, laughing.

I then found out more about Sadie by asking her about her interests.

"What hobbies and interests do you have?"

"I like languages, music, travelling and animals."

"Another animal lover. That's good to hear. Do you watch many wildlife programmes on television?"

"I try to watch as many as I can, especially on the BBC. They have so many good shows on. I have recently been watching *Autumn Watch*, which I have enjoyed," said Sadie.

"I like that too. Did you see the wildlife series *Planet Earth II*?"

"Oh, yes I have watched all the six episodes. They have been great, so many stunning images."

"What have you enjoyed the most?" I said.

"I have loved the scenes with the snow leopards. They are such beautiful animals."

"They are lovely animals but very rare. Not many people have seen them and they haven't been filmed much. I heard that they used these special motion cameras to film the leopards when they moved. Lots of cameras were put in the areas where they lived and when they moved, the cameras filmed them. The technology is so good these days," I added.

"What have you liked the most?" asked Sadie.

"There have been so many memorable scenes that I find it difficult to pick a favourite. I must admit I don't really like to see animals kill other animals but I do have an admiration for the jaguar. The film of the jaguar killing the ten-foot long caiman, which is also a fearsome predator, was very impressive."

"Yes, that was impressive. What I like about the film is that it shows how nature gives every animal, bird and insect a fair chance of survival," said Sadie.

"You're right. Nature is incredible in that sense. A good example of that is when they show the tree lizard being cornered by another lizard in a tall tree. It reaches the end of a branch and you think it has no chance. However, it produces wings and floats away onto another tree. That's an amazing scene. Did you say you like travelling as well?"

"Yes I am intending to visit several countries in Europe next spring."

"Which countries are you going to?"

"Germany, Poland and Austria. I want to improve my German so travelling to these countries should help me."

"Are you going with anyone?"

"My best friend is going with me. We shall try to get jobs to pay our way out there. We hope to stay for a month in each country."

"That should be exciting," I stated.

"I am looking forward to it."

"I have an idea, what about if you sent me pictures of all these places you visit and a report so I can put them in the newsletter? Everyone at the shop can follow your adventures."

"Are you not on Facebook?"

"No, I am not. I also think that people like Rita and Belinda aren't on Facebook."

"All right, I could do that," said Sadie.

"I will give you my email address before you go."

Then Belinda called Sadie over to give her some work to do in the front storeroom. I thought that it was amazing that so many workers at this shop have had work problems. It's as if this shop attracts these vulnerable workers and helps them.

Chapter 11

It was a week before Halloween and I had finished the latest newsletter, a Halloween paranormal special. I had been doing these newsletters since June so this would be the fifth one. I enjoyed doing them. I had been doing similar newsletters at two different companies for the last ten years. I mainly did them about news at the companies but I included joke pages (including jokes I made up myself), interesting articles and, cartoons. I also did special editions, about sport in general, the Olympic Games, football World Cups, the paranormal, animals, the environment, a couple of best of British issues and several Christmas issues. I mainly did these myself but I did get some help from a few workers at these companies.

There were usually about six workmates in each of these places who read them. They were popular.

These RSPCA newsletters are slightly different to my old ones. I still include news (at the shop), cartoons, joke pages and articles. However, the differences include the monthly bar chart sales figures for Saturdays (the average for the month), a Room 101 feature of people's pet hates and also the animal fact-file, a focus on a different animal each month.

This Halloween special has extra features on the history of Halloween, a scary story by Grace, my favourite horror films, my paranormal experiences, a profile on Peter Cushing, one of my favourite horror film actors and a funny cartoon about a ghostly sighting of a woman in the front storeroom. I had some help doing these newsletters from Grace, the young volunteer.

Grace has contributed features such as the animal fact-files since July and they have all been excellent. I have let her have the freedom to choose any animal. She has chosen animals as diverse as zebras, scorpions, corn snakes and bats. She has also done Room 101 features on her pet hates, which have been witty and insightful.

For this Halloween special, Grace did another animal fact-file, a very good Room 101 on her Halloween pet hates and most impressively of all, a scary story about a rabbit who gained its revenge on its owners who had neglected it. Grace is a talented writer and I was very impressed with this story.

I had seen Grace's early efforts for the newsletter and seen how good she was. She has an edge to her writing which I like. She is witty and sharp. So I encouraged her to do more articles. She has told me that she enjoys doing them. As a result, I have made her my assistant editor, which has pleased her a lot. She takes the job quite seriously and sends her articles and features to me by email, by the deadlines I set.

When I returned to the shop after my break at 2:00 p.m., I gave Grace a copy of the finished newsletter.

"Hi, Grace, how are you?"

"Fine, thanks, Greg."

"I have finished the latest newsletter. Here's your copy."

"Oh, great."

She skimmed through it, "I was just checking to see what my pieces look like."

"Your articles and features are very good, especially the animal fact-file about the bat. It fitted in well with the Halloween theme."

"Glad you liked it."

"Also your scary story about the revengeful rabbit was excellent. It was so well written."

"Thanks. I enjoyed doing it. I have a vivid imagination."

"Have you written stories like this before?" I asked.

"Yes. I have done a few short stories before but not for newsletters or for publication."

"I like your style of writing. You are so sharp and witty...it shows up well when you do the Room 101's."

"Thanks."

"I have done a funny cartoon about a ghostly woman who appears in the front store room in this issue. It is a picture of you. Hope you like it."

"I didn't notice that. Let me have a quick look. Oh, yes. It's funny. I like it."

"Remember when I took that picture of the Halloween display. I took a couple of you as well."

"I remember it. I think I am going to take a picture of it and put it on my Facebook page," said Grace.

"It's strange because I had planned to do this joke about you but when the picture developed there was a white shadow on it which makes the picture more spooky and atmospheric."

"It does look much better with the white streak on. You use an old type of camera, don't you?" said Grace.

"Yes. I prefer them. Normally, I don't have many problems getting them developed."

"Maybe fate intervened."

"I reckon it's the best newsletter we have done so far. I am very pleased with it."

"It does look very good."

"It's going to be difficult to improve on it."

"We shall have to try," said Grace.

"I shall e-mail you this weekend to let you know what you can do for the next issue. I will give you a deadline. I shall get it printed about the middle of next month. That will give us about four weeks to get it finished, probably around four weekends."

"OK. I usually do my articles and features on Sundays when I have a spare bit of time. I enjoy doing them."

"That's good. I don't want to give you too much work and put you under pressure," I said.

"I enjoy writing. They are a challenge to me," replied Grace.

"I am going to have this weekend off from doing the newsletter and should be refreshed enough to start work on the next one, next weekend."

"All right."

"I had better let you get on with your work."

Grace started to open a bag of women's clothes that were donated and began sorting through them. I went back out into the shop.

I took over at the till in order to give Sadie a break. She went over the road to the chip shop to buy some chips while I took over.

A little later, Sadie came back out after her meal and told me that the man in the chip shop had had a problem with a man threatening them with a knife, earlier in the week.

"This strange man had been threatening the shop owner," said Sadie.

"He sounds a nasty piece of work."

"Yes, this was the second time he has been causing trouble."

"Have they reported him to the police?"

"Yes, but they were reluctant to do anything."

"They should because he could stab someone. He might be mentally ill."

"The shopkeeper doesn't know what to do," said Sadie.

"Isn't he on the intercom system that we use in this shop?"

"No, he's not."

"Perhaps the best thing he could do is contact the security man at Iceland to find out how to get on this Intercom system and ask him for some advice on what to do," I added.

"Yes, I will after I finish work."

"Most of the shops in this area have an intercom system where shop workers can report any suspicious customers or actual shoplifters. They would describe the person's appearance and this would be a warning to other shop workers to look out for them," I stated.

"I see."

"Perhaps I had better show you our secret weapon against shoplifters and violent customers."

"What's that?" said Sadie.

"This I said," pulling out a baseball bat from under the till.

"Wow! I didn't know you had that."

"This can be used as a last resort. The best action to take is if there are any violent people in the shop, ring the bell to get someone out to help you. If I am around on the shop floor call me over."

"All right," said Sadie.

"Hopefully, we won't have any trouble makers in but you never know. It's better to be prepared."

Chapter 12

Halloween was over and the display was taken down. In its place was the Christmas display.

This consisted of a Christmas tree, a couple of Father Christmases and many decorations. It seemed strange that Christmas items should be put out in early November but I suppose it gave customers plenty of time to buy these Christmas goods.

The Bric-à-brac was moved to another shelf and fewer items were put out. The two shelves left empty from the Bric-à-brac were filled with Christmas goods, including decorations, gift tags, gift bags and Christmas cuddly toys.

The RSPCA Christmas cards and calendars were put out near the counter. I bought one set of Christmas cards which had a lovely design of a couple I walking in the snow. I also bought a British wildlife calendar, which had a different British animal for each month.

Shortly after starting work, Belinda told me that a man had applied to be a volunteer but she had turned his application down.

"Why did you reject him?" I asked.

"There was something about him that I didn't like," said Belinda.

"Did he look rough?"

"Yes, he did. He didn't dress that well for the interview. I don't always judge a book by its cover but he made me feel uneasy."

"I understand."

"I have to take into account whether new volunteers will get on with each other. I think he would cause me problems. He was also an hour late."

"He wouldn't be any good then, if he turned up that late."

"He was also looking around my office a lot, showing too much interest in what I had in it."

"I got the feeling that he had come here to be a volunteer because his job centre had told him he had to otherwise he might be sanctioned and his benefit might be stopped. He doesn't seem the type of person to want to do anything for free unless he has to," added Belinda.

"I think you have done the right thing. I doubt if I would have got on with him. Oh, I nearly forgot. Do you remember the black and grey jumper I bought last Saturday?"

"Yes, I remember selling you it."

"I washed it at the weekend and it has shrunk from a man's medium size to a child's size."

"Has it?" said Belinda, laughing.

"I bought it in to show you. It's in my bag. I will fetch it."

"OK. I have got to see this."

When I bought it out to show Belinda, she burst into laughter. The jumper looked like it was a child's one.

"It's my fault because I didn't look at the washing instructions. It says wash it in cold water."

"That's unusual for clothes. Normally, you wash them in hot water," said Belinda.

"Can I have a refund?" I said, laughing.

"No!" said Belinda firmly. "It's your fault. We could sell it as a boy's jumper though."

"OK," I said, laughing.

"OK, Greg. Can you take over the till while I go out to the chemist to buy some paracetamol? I have a terrible headache."

"Yes, I will take over."

I thought about what Belinda had said about that man who wanted to be a volunteer and thought how lucky we were at this shop to have such nice people to work with.

Sharon then came onto the shop to put out some new stock of women's clothes. After she had finished, I spoke to her.

"How are you, Sharon? I haven't seen you for a while on Saturdays."

"Not too bad, Greg, I haven't been needed much since Sadie has started here."

"Yes, she has been good. Didn't you have a problem with your bank account? Belinda told me about it."

"I had a problem last week. I withdrew some money one day and then a few days later I discovered that £127 had been taken out my account."

"How did you find out?"

"When I came to pay my rent, I had gone overdrawn and I didn't have enough money to pay it."

"What did you do?"

"I had to borrow it from my mom. I didn't want to ask her but I needed it."

"Don't you have an overdraft facility?"

"I do but I was overdrawn when the money was taken so I went into emergency borrowing which the bank will charge me for."

"I understand. Did you not cover your hand when you tapped your number in?" I asked.

"No, I didn't."

"I think it's best to do this. There might be a hidden camera there."

"I now go inside the bank and use the cashpoints inside," stated Sharon.

"It's hard to know how these thieves got your money," I said.

"I have been told that thieves can get your card details from a machine in their pockets."

"Oh, yes I have heard this too. Will your bank give you this money back?"

"They have said they will but they are slow in doing it."

Suddenly, we had a problem with a female customer who had come to the till to be served. She had terrible body odour. It was as if she hadn't had a shower or bath for two weeks. After I had served her, I asked Sharon to get an air freshener out so we could spray the shop. Most of our customers were clean and well dressed, but occasionally we had a few bad ones in. Sharon came back fairly quickly and gave the shop a good spray. The smell was much sweeter now. Sharon smiled as she went back into the front storeroom.

A regular customer came in the shop then and spoke to me. He mentioned the work being done by workmen in the town.

"How are things?" he asked.

"A bit slow today. I think it's all the work being done in the town on the pavements and roads."

"Yes, there are too many delays and traffic jams."

"I think people are avoiding the area if they have to come by car. We are still getting local people in who can walk here but people who live far away are staying away."

"I am looking for a coat. Have you got many winter coats in?"

"We have been putting some winter coats out for men and women in the last few weeks," I said.

"OK. I will have a look around."

Belinda returned from the chemists and took a few paracetamol pills. She then came out to talk to me about the bowling night that Adam had organised for early December.

"Are you interested in going to this bowling night on December 10th? It will be in Birmingham," said Belinda.

"I haven't played for about ten years but I will give it a try."

"I think most of us haven't played for a while. Only Adam plays it regularly."

"Who's going then?"

"Adam, Grace, Sharon, Sadie, Maxine from the week and me. So if you come there will be seven of us."

"How much is it?"

"Six pounds. This will include the booking for the alley and for the taxi there and back."

"All right. Put me down for it. When do I have to pay?"

"You are all right until early December. It should be a good night out and good for morale," said Belinda.

"Yes, it should be good for us to socialise," I agreed.

Belinda then went to her office to have a sit down while I worked on the till. More customers had come in and sales were picking up.

Later on, at around 3:30 p.m., Belinda told me she was going to shut the shop because she wasn't feeling too well. She must have been bad because this was the first time I had known her do this. Fortunately, we had over £200 worth of sales so it would be all right. I said to her that I hoped she would be better soon.

Chapter 13

It was the night of the bowling. There were seven of us going, including Belinda, Grace, Adam, Sadie, Sharon, Maxine and me. I was a bit apprehensive because I hadn't played for over ten years and I was worried I might make a fool of myself. Fortunately for me, most of the others hadn't played for years either. Only Adam played the game regularly. So, there would be competition to finish second.

We had agreed to meet outside the shop between 7:15 p.m. and 7:30 p.m. so a taxi could collect us and take us there. I was the first there. Sharon came second and we chatted about her recent problem with her bank. This concerned money going out from her account a few weeks before. Thankfully, her bank had reimbursed her. Adam came next. He didn't wear a coat despite it being quite cold and wet. Adam was in his mid-thirties, quite big and dressed for comfort in baggy jeans and a T-shirt rather than to look good.

The rest of the group soon arrived and the taxi came not long after. Soon, we were at the bowling complex. Most of us were wearing training shoes or soft soled shoes, which were suitable for playing but Belinda and myself didn't have any so we wore a pair of special shoes that they had there.

We were put next to a team of men who looked like they were experienced at the game. They were throwing the ball down the alley at great speeds. Just what we didn't want as most of us hadn't played for years and were very rusty.

We were split into two teams. Adam, Belinda, Maxine and I were in one team and Grace, Sharon and Sadie were in the other.

I got off to a great start when I had a clean strike, knocking all the skittles down with my first throw. I think it was just luck because I didn't do it again in any of the other nine subsequent throws. The best I did after that was to knock down eight of the skittles a few times and then I needed a second go to knock the rest of them over. I had found a favourite red ball which was the right weight for me and the correct hole size for my fingers and I kept using this.

Adam was doing very well. He had about three clean strikes. He played it regularly so it was not too surprising. Belinda and Maxine did reasonably well. They both had good run ups and threw the ball quite straight. Our team was the better out the two teams.

While waiting for my turn, I watched the other team. Sharon was probably the best, hitting more of the skittles than the others. I couldn't believe how bad Grace was. She walked up to the line and threw the ball with a round-arm action, which caused the ball to go too far to the right most of the time and miss most of the skittles. After seeing her do this several times, Adam and I gave Grace a few tips but she couldn't improve and finished last. She said her hand-eye coordination was not good.

The winner was Adam with 126 points. I came second with 86 points and Maxine was third with 60 points. Adam had won it easily. I felt as if I could get better if I went more often. Adam collected his prize of £10. We said we would do it again.

After the bowling, we had a drink together and then played a game of pool. This was not my type of game at all. I am an outdoor sports person, not an indoor one. I have hardly ever played it so I didn't expect to do well. When I was paired up with Grace for a doubles match, I knew we were going to do badly. It was like asking us to play tennis against Andy Murray and his brother, Jamie. We would have no chance of doing well.

We were due to play Adam, another indoor sport he was good at, and Sadie. I hit a couple of the right balls in the hole but I also hit a couple of wrong balls in the hole. Grace was even worse than me. She couldn't hit the ball in a straight line.

It wasn't long before Adam and Sadie beat us. They played Belinda and Sharon in the final.

While this pool match was going on, I spoke to Grace about sport and whether she was any good at it.

"Are you good at any sports?"

"I was no good at them at school. I have bad hand-eye coordination and I don't like any sports."

"I bet you were not too popular at games when sides were picked for football, netball and so on."

"I was always picked last if I was at games."

"Did you have a lot of time off school?"

"Yes. I used to take a lot of sick notes in," said Grace.

"I was the opposite, I was good at sport and I used to love playing football, cricket and running. I was good at them as well, in all the school teams," I said.

"You look quite fit. What was your favourite sport?"

"I used to like football and running. I was a fast runner at the 100m and 200m."

"Were you competitive?"

"Yes, I was. I always wanted to win."

"You don't seem like that now," said Grace.

"No. I suppose as I have got older, I don't always want to win as much. If you weren't good at sport, what were you good at, at school? Was it English?"

"That was one my favourite subjects at school, along with art."

"Did you like writing stories then?"

"I started writing stories quite early," answered Grace.

"You certainly write well. So, you were good at art as well. You are quite an artistic person."

"I paint as well as write."

"You are a talented woman. You must send me some of your paintings and I can include some in the newsletter."

"OK. I will send you some over when I get some time."

"I could do a feature called 'The RSPCA's Got Talent', similar to the television programme. I did something like this before when I was working at my last place."

"Were there some talented people there?"

"Yes. Even though it was a factory, one woman painted landscapes and another could draw portraits of people. I included one example from each of them. They were very good," I added.

The pool game was nearly finished. Adam and Sadie looked like they were on the verge of winning with only a few balls left to pot.

I then took a chance with Grace and asked her what she was doing afterwards.

"What are you doing after?"

"Nothing really. I was intending to go home."

"What about going for a drink in Brindley Place? It's just up the road," I said.

"You mean with some of the others?"

"I meant just us two."

Grace smiled and said, "I thought you would never ask."

I then smiled, saying, "You mean you want to go for a drink?"

"Yes."

"Great. I was a bit apprehensive about asking you out because I didn't want to ruin our friendship. I have liked you for a while."

"I know. Women can usually tell when a man likes us. What do you like about me?"

"Most things. You are very attractive but you have some very good qualities."

"Like what."

"You are friendly, artistic, talented, caring, hardworking, and serious about many issues but you do have a nice sense of humour."

"That's nice of you to say."

"In fact, if you were rich, you would be my ideal woman," I added, laughing.

"I hope you are joking," she said, laughing.

"I'm only joking. Are you not worried about the twenty-year age gap?"

"Not really. I am very mature for my age and you are a bit immature for your age so we meet in the middle," said Grace, laughing.

"Thanks a lot," I said, laughing. "Shall we go now before the others notice?"

"OK. I had better tell Belinda that I am getting a bus home. We could have one drink together. I don't want to get home too late."

"That sounds all right to me."

Chapter 14

It was Christmas Eve and everybody was in a cheerful mood. Rita, Sadie, Indiana and me turned up but, unfortunately, Grace had rung in to say that she needed to do some Christmas shopping and wouldn't be coming in. This was disappointing for me because I always enjoyed working with her. Also, since the night of the bowling when we both went for a drink afterwards, I had been getting on well with her. We had suggested going out somewhere during the Christmas break. I think we were making progress. There was a mutual respect for each other, a chemistry between us and we had many things in common. Belinda had started her holidays in order to use them all up before the end of January.

Rita had brought in her daughter's lovely Jack Russell dog, Jack. This dog always attracted a lot of attention from the customers. He was so friendly that he would run up to every customer to be stroked.

I jokingly said to one man, "You have to stroke him on the way in and on the way out."

"Yes, he's a lovely dog, really friendly," said the man.

"He loves people," I said.

"I can see that. He has a lovely temperament."

"He very rarely barks. He's not for sale, though."

"That's a pity. I would be tempted to buy him if he was," said the man laughing as he left the shop.

Rita had left out Christmas presents for all the volunteers from herself and Belinda. There were also lots of Christmas cards left out for everyone on the kitchen table. In addition, there were mince pies and shortbread left out for everyone to eat on their breaks.

Even though Grace wasn't there, I still had a good time working with Sadie. We worked well on the till together, talking about many things and having a laugh and a joke. She was one of these people who brought the best out of me in terms of witty sayings and jokes.

Surprisingly enough, there were plenty of customers in and sales of Christmas items were going very well. One woman bought in a bag to donate. As she was signing up to become a Gift Aid person, I looked through it. There were a few paperback books in there which I took out to put prices on to put out on the shelves as we were going low on our stocks of paperback novels. Also in this bag were several books about foreign languages, including a book on German. I thought this would be suitable for Sadie. So when she finished signing up this woman for Gift Aid, I showed her it.

"Look what that woman donated," I said and showed her the German language book.

"Oh great. I will have that."

"It's amazing how this shop seems to produce things that we need," I said to Sadie.

A man came in the shop to return a suit he had recently bought. The trousers were too short. I had served him earlier and had asked him about the fit but he said he would be all right. We had to call Rita out to deal with him. She couldn't give him a refund. Instead, she gave him a credit note for £25, the full value of the item. He can then buy other items to the value of this amount within the next month. I explained to Rita that I had asked him if he had tried the suit on. Rita replied that it was the customer's fault if he didn't try the clothes on. There is a changing room available to them.

In mid-afternoon, Rita went out to empty the clothing and shoe bank situated outside the shop. This was for people to donate clothes and shoes when the shop was shut. Sometimes, people put other things in there.

Rita came running in to tell me that the lock had gone missing. I went out with her to have a look but neither of us could find the lock. Rita suspected that someone had stolen it. We both emptied it. It was mostly clothes but I did find two video cassettes and some Christmas lights. I threw away the video cassettes because no one would buy them these days.

Rita had to buy another lock from the shop across the road. She fitted the new lock safely. Panic over.

Shortly afterwards, when I was taking a break with Rita, while having a drink and eating a mince pie, we spoke about the missing lock.

"It's a strange situation. I have never known the lock to go missing and I have worked here for nearly 10 years."

"Could someone have misplaced it," I said.

"It's possible. Maybe someone left it on the top of the clothing bank and someone took it. I have told Belinda about it. She can ask some of the other volunteers if they know where it is."

"There seems to be a fair amount of rubbish put in there. I found two video cassettes and Christmas lights."

"We mainly allow clothes and shoes but if people put books, DVDs and CDs in bags, that will be all right."

"So there is a little bit of leeway for people to donate other things."

"Yes, but we have to be careful that it's not used as a rubbish bin. Those video cassettes shouldn't have been put in there because we can't sell them and there isn't a market for them."

"I see."

"Also, we have to be careful to empty the clothing bank regularly because it can fill up fairly quickly and if it gets overfull this encourages some people to steal items from there," added Rita.

"Do people steal things from it?"

"Oh, yes. I have seen sticks and rods left in the clothing bank from when people have been trying to steal items out there and the sticks have fallen in."

"I didn't think people would do that from a charity clothing bank."

"Belinda has caught a woman stealing from there early in the morning. This woman was putting the clothes in her shopping bag."

"What did Belinda do?"

"She threatened to call the police if this woman didn't put them back, which she did."

Just then Grace appeared. She said she had finished her Christmas shopping earlier than she had expected and came in for the last hour and a half. I made her some tea and gave her a mince pie.

"I thought you wouldn't have come in this late," I said.

"I missed it," said Grace munching on a mince pie.

"It's good to see you. Oh, thanks for your Christmas card."

"That's OK. Thanks for your card and also the present. That was a nice message you wrote in my card."

"I wanted to thank you for contributing so many good articles to the newsletter," I said.

"I have enjoyed doing them. I am looking forward to opening my present on Christmas Day."

"It's just a small present."

"Small things can be good. Right, I shall open a few bags and get some work ready for Tuesday," said Grace.

"All right I shall see you a bit later. I shall see if Rita needs anything doing in the shop."

I then went back out to the shop to see what was going on. It was starting to slow down. There weren't many customers in.

A little later, I went in the back to find Grace trying on a pair of black trousers she had spotted in one of the donated bags. They were quite baggy and seemed to have two layers. Grace has a lovely figure but they didn't show it off. Grace asked me what I thought of them. I had to be honest and said I didn't like them. She agreed saying they didn't look good or feel that comfortable to wear. Even a supermodel would struggle to look good in them, I thought.

It was time to finish. Surprisingly, sales were quite good, £239.28, which was good for this time shortly before Christmas when so many people go into Birmingham or shop online. Sadie left first. I wished her a merry Christmas and a

Happy New Year. As the following Saturday was on New Year's Eve, the shop wouldn't be opening until next year.

While Rita was cashing up in the shop, I asked Grace if she still wanted to meet up during Christmas.

"Do you still want to meet up during Christmas for a drink, Grace?"

"Yes. That should be nice."

"OK. I will text you to fix up a date and time."

Chapter 15

I reached the 'Slug & Lettuce' pub at the Water's Edge in Brindley Place, Birmingham at 2:35 p.m. I was 25 minutes early for my date with Grace. I had set off early to avoid all the heavy traffic that would be on the roads. Even though it was Tuesday, it was the day after Boxing Day so there would be lots of people on holiday from work. This was my first real date with Grace and I didn't want anything to go wrong. I had gone for a drink with her after the bowling night but that wasn't a proper date. I had dressed up in my best clothes, black trousers, black striped shirt and my warmest winter coat. I wanted to create a good impression.

I looked around the pub. It was a pleasant, family pub that served a wide variety of drinks, including real ale. It also served food. The customers were fairly mixed. There were several families with young children having meals, couples on dates and groups of friends out for a few drinks. I found myself a nice comfortable seat away from the door and waited for Grace. I didn't have to wait too long. Grace appeared about ten minutes after me. She was also early.

I beckoned her over, stood up and smiled at her. She looked lovely. She was wearing a red coat, that complemented her red hair, a blue top and blue jeans that showed off her wonderful figure.

"Hi, Grace, how are you?"

"Fine, thanks. I had hoped to get here before you."

"Ha-ha. I beat you to it," I said laughing.

"I'm usually the earliest on dates. How was your Christmas, Greg?"

"It was fairly quiet but I had an enjoyable time. I saw my sister and her family on Christmas Day and my brother on Boxing Day. What about your Christmas?"

"My Christmas was similar to yours. I spent it with my family. I was at my mom's house for Christmas Day and Boxing Day, seeing my mom, my dad and my sister. We had some really nice meals and saw some good television programmes."

"You didn't have turkey, did you?"

"Yes. I quite like it. It was nice with roast vegetables. What did you have?"

"I had a really nice vegetarian ready meal along with lots of roast vegetables for Christmas Day and stuffed peppers and other vegetables for Boxing Day. They were very appetising," I answered.

"Thanks for your presents. I love that brooch of the bird and that CD of 'The Smiths Greatest Hits' is very good. I can see why you like them so much. Their songs are so melodic, witty and controversial."

"I'm glad you like the presents. I've always loved The Smiths music, it's timeless. As good now as it was in the 1980s. Thanks for the chocolate. I love mint Matchmakers."

"I remember you saying how much you like chocolate, especially Matchmakers."

"It's nice to get a Christmas present I like. I sometimes have to donate my unwanted presents to the shop."

"I have had plenty of bad Christmas presents as well. I remember once I had a box of cheap perfume. It smelt awful. As I had opened it, I had to give it to my sister. What bad presents have you had?"

"I remember one Christmas my brother gave me this book about ancient maps. It was so boring. I donated it to a charity shop. All right, what drink do you want?"

"I'll have a coke, please."

I went to the bar to buy some drinks.

When I returned with our drinks, I gave Grace her coke and I had a lager. She seemed relaxed and happy. She had taken her coat off and looked stunning, her big hazel eyes beaming.

"Thanks, what did you think about the Secret Santa at the shop?" said Grace.

"I was disappointed in it. I received a boy's toy, a Transformer toy. I think someone did this as a practical joke."

"Who do you think sent it?"

"I think it was probably Adam, knowing his sense of humour. What did you get?"

"I had a couple of good presents, a mug with the slogan 'Hippy Chick' on and some chocolate. They were fairly cheap but all right."

"I wish someone had given me chocolate. It's the first time I have taken part in a Secret Santa and it will be the last. I have never really understood the thinking behind it. Why would you send someone a Christmas present without letting them know you sent it?"

"I have always enjoyed them but you can get a bad present sometimes," replied Grace.

It went a bit quiet then for a while. We both sipped our drinks and looked around. We both smiled at each other. Despite this silence, we were comfortable with each other and didn't mind the quiet moments. It was probably because we had worked with each other for so long. I broke the silence by asking her about her taste in music.

"What type of music do you like?"

"I mainly like pop, rock, a bit of heavy metal and RnB music. I don't like rap or grime. What about you?"

"I'm a bit like that as well. I don't like rap or grime music but I do have a wide taste in music. I like rock, pop, punk, soul, some reggae and some classical music."

"Do you like much music from the past?" inquired Grace.

"Yes. I like '60s' stuff from The Beatles, The Kinks and The Who, '70s' music by The Jam, The Police, Kate Bush, The Buzzcocks and Blondie, '80s' music by The Smiths, The Pretenders, Tears for Fears and XTC I think good pop and rock music, like classical music, doesn't date. It still sounds good today."

"I'm going back further into the past and discovering great music as well."

"You have got YouTube, old episodes of '*Top of The Pops*' on BBC4 and also all the documentaries on bands on BBC4. I'm quite knowledgeable about music but even I find out new things about bands and artists."

"When are you going back to work, Grace?"

"I have taken an extra day off that was due to me so I go back on Thursday, the 29th, I think. I lose track of the dates."

"I know what you mean. When you are on holiday, you do tend to forget about the days and the dates. I have longer than you. I go back next Monday, January the 2nd."

"Lucky you. I suppose I have to expect short holidays when I work at a shop."

"Are you doing much for New Year's Eve?" I asked.

"I haven't made any definite plans. I used to go to the city centre for the fireworks with my friends when I was younger but I haven't been for a while. Have you got any plans?"

"No, not yet. What about us meeting up on New Year's Eve to celebrate in the city centre, just like you used to in the old days?"

"That sounds good."

"Great," I said.

The pub suddenly became very crowded and noisy. I was struggling to make myself heard and I could see that Grace was getting annoyed. I then decided to ask Grace if she wanted to have a walk by the canal. "Do you want to get out of here and take a walk?"

"Yes. That would be good. It's getting too loud in here."

"All right, we could walk along the canal and then work our way to the city centre."

"I also want to have a look at all the Christmas decorations. They always look good in the dark," replied Grace.

We put our coats back on and made our way out of the pub. The weather was cold and dry and it was getting quite dark. We walked past the bars and restaurants along the canal, all lit up and sparkling. After a while, Grace linked her arm with mine. I didn't say anything but I was pleased. We made our way onto Broad Street by the ICC. Outside the building was a poster for a Ray Davies concert which was due to take place in March next year. I stopped to read it.

"Are you a big fan of him?" enquired Grace.

"Yes, I am. He was the lead singer and main songwriter of The Kinks from the '60s and '70s. I've always liked the group."

"Remind me of some of their best songs."

"You have probably heard of *Waterloo Sunset*, *Lola* and *You Really Got Me*."

"I have heard of the first two. They are very good songs."

"Are you interested in going to see him live? He'll probably play a lot of the old hits."

"I'm not sure. We can find out what day it's on."

"My birthday is in March so it could be a good night out for my birthday," I added.

"All right. We'll make some enquiries about it. I haven't been to see a live band or singer for a long while."

We then turned towards the city centre, walking past the Birmingham REP and the new library, two of my favourite places in Birmingham. The library looked wonderful with its distinctive building, resembling a birthday cake. It sparkled in the darkening sky.

"When is your birthday?" I asked.

"Next month, the 17th."

"Ah, so, it's quite close. I shall have to think up a good present to give you," I replied.

"I was thinking that as I like charity shops, I could go to each one in Marwood and buy something from each one. That would be a good birthday present from you to me."

"What do you mean! There are 7 charity shops there," I said quite shocked.

"I know but I could have a limit. I'm not too expensive."

"All right, as long as you come with me to the Ray Davies concert."

"Mmm. OK. It's a deal."

"Good. Perhaps we can have a limit for you of £15?" I said hopefully.

"No, let's make it £20."

"You drive a hard bargain."

"Ha-ha," said Grace.

We continued walking towards the city centre, past the Birmingham Council House and Birmingham Art Gallery. Grace had still got her arm linked with mine. I then took her hand and held it as we approached New Street. She allowed me to hold her hand.

"The Christmas decorations look so lovely, don't they?" said Grace.

"They do. I was thinking about us. Shall we keep our relationship from the rest of the volunteers?"

"Yes, for a while. Let's see how things go for a few months."

"All right. We can keep things quiet."

Then Grace asked me some questions about myself.

"I know you like sport, reading, music and animals but what other interests do you have?" asked Grace.

"Since I lost my job and my house a couple of years ago, I tend to like the simple things in life now, walking in parks, going on day trips to places like Malvern Hills and Clent Hills to see the beautiful countryside and also watching television programmes."

"Oh, you like walking in parks. Marwood has some good ones. There's a good park near me as well which I go running in."

"Yes. I'm lucky to live so close to these two excellent parks. On weekends and during holidays, I always try to go walking in these places. I feel invigorated after a long brisk walk, seeing all the trees and greenery. When I work, I get enough exercise because my job is fairly active. Sundays, in particular, I like to take a walk in one of these parks before going to the shops."

"As I get older, I can see what you mean about parks and the countryside. When you live in towns and cities, you can get a bit stressed out so it's nice to get away from all the noise, pollution and people."

"That's exactly how I feel so you go jogging? I can see why you have such a lovely figure?"

"I try to keep in shape. I mainly jog at weekends when I don't work."

"I was good at sports when I was young but I was never any good at long distance running so I wouldn't be any good at jogging. I think brisk walking is just as good."

Grace then said she wanted to go home. It was getting on for 8:00 p.m. and it was getting much colder. I walked her to Colmore Row to get her bus back home.

"Where shall we meet up on New Year's Eve?" I asked.

"What about outside Waterstones at 7:00 p.m.?"

"All right. See you then."

Grace's bus appeared almost immediately. Before she left she told me that she had a great time and thanked me. I told her I had enjoyed myself too. I then caught my bus back to Marwood.

Chapter 16

It was the first Saturday in the New Year and I made my way into the shop at 10:30 a.m. I was glad to be back after the Christmas and New Year holiday. It would be nice to see all the workers at the shop again, Belinda, Sadie, Rita and of course, Grace.

Belinda was on the till when I arrived. She said good morning to me as I went in the Front storeroom. Sadie was already there sorting through some bags of donations.

"Hi, Sadie, how are you?"

"All right, thanks. What about you?"

"I'm fine too. Did you have a good Christmas?"

"Yes. It was great. I went to a lot of parties and had a great time. What about you?"

"It was fairly quiet, I spent it with my sister and brother but I did have a good time."

"Have you heard that Rita is leaving? Her husband has recently had a hip operation and she needs to look after him."

"I didn't know about that."

"I didn't until I came in. Belinda told me when I came in earlier. I think Rita is also looking forward to retiring early as she is now 60."

"That's a shame because I have always got on well with Rita," I said.

"Yes. I like her too. She was very kind and helpful to me when I first started. I will miss her."

"I had better go out to see Belinda to see what she wants me to do," I stated.

When I went out into the shop, Belinda asked me to empty the clothing bank outside the shop because it would be full after the holidays. I went away to get the key to the lock of the clothing bank and fetch several large bags to put the clothes and other items in. When I opened it, there was the usual mixture of good quality clothes and shoes but also some rubbish such as used perfume bottles, opened shampoo bottles and some used insoles for shoes. We wouldn't be able to sell these items. I had to throw them away. After taking six full bags into the shop and writing on the bags 'Clothing Bank', Belinda asked Sadie to take over from her on the till. She wanted to talk to me about Rita leaving.

"You have probably heard that Rita is going to leave," said Belinda.

"Yes, Sadie told me. It's a pity she's going. I've got on well with her."

"I don't think she has a choice. Her husband has recently had a hip operation and he needs a lot of care. I think she also wants to give up the job. Rita has worked here about 10 years and I think she has had enough."

"I understand. Who's going to replace her?" I inquired. "I have already asked Sharon and Adam but neither are interested in the job. I was going to ask you and Grace if you wanted to apply for the job."

"It's nice of you to ask. I think I'm too inexperienced at working at charity shops. I've only been here a year. Grace might be more suitable. She's been here longer, two years."

"Yes. I think you could be right," said Belinda. "I will ask her when she comes in later in the afternoon. I would prefer to work with someone I know and get on with. I did have a bad experience before when a new assistant manager worked with me. She was from another shop and was used to doing things differently to me and this shop. We clashed a lot. After six months of conflict, she finally went back to her old job at the RSPCA shop in Birmingham."

Belinda went back to work on the till and I went in the back to sort some books out to fill up the gaps in the bookshelves. It was my favourite job in the shop. I have always loved reading and handling books. I was really pleased that the sales of books had increased in recent weeks to over £10 on most Saturdays.

When I returned from my break at 2:00 p.m. Grace called me over to discuss the situation about the vacancy for Rita's old job.

"Hi, Greg, Belinda has asked me if I am interested in applying for Rita's old job."

"Yes, she told me she would ask you. What did you say?"

"I've told her I would like the job."

"That's great. I think you would do a good job."

"Thanks. The interviews are taking place next Friday morning at head office in Birmingham. I will take the morning off at my job."

"Who else has applied for the job?"

"Belinda has told me that two volunteers from other RSPCA shops have shown interest and will attend the interviews. Belinda doesn't know them."

"You should have a good chance of getting it. Belinda rates you highly. You have been here two years and you can do nearly every job at the shop."

"I haven't cashed up here yet but I have done it a few times at the shop I work at."

"Belinda did say she would have a big influence in who takes over. You might have a slight advantage."

"I think I have a good chance but I can't be too confident. I'm a bit nervous. I'm not looking forward to it. I have never liked job interviews."

"Good luck. I hope you get it."

"Thanks. I'll need it."

I then went out to work on the till to give Belinda a break. Grace continued to sort through bags of donations. When I arrived at the till, Belinda told me about a strange customer she had in earlier.

"This woman came into the shop and took two tops into the changing room. I thought she was going to try them on but when she came out, she was wearing a Little Red Riding Hood fancy dress outfit."

"That's very odd."

"Then she asked me to take a picture of her."

"What! I can't believe it."

"I refused and told her off for using the changing room for her own personal use. There were two other women waiting and I said she was taking up the changing room when others wanted to use it."

"What did she say?"

"She was amazed that I wouldn't take her picture. She stormed off." Belinda added.

"That woman had a cheek. Was she a regular customer?"

"I have seen her in here before a few times but she's not a regular customer."

Belinda then went off to get a drink and have a break. A woman then came to the till to buy a coat that was reduced to half price in a sale. She was very pleased to buy it until she noticed a slight fault in it at the last minute. A few stiches in the arm had come away. She was unsure whether to go ahead with buying it until she finally said she would buy it. I told her not to worry if these stitches come away to reveal a hole because she could start a trend for ripped coats. This amused her.

It then went quiet for about 10 minutes. No one came in at all. I looked around the shop at some of the new donations. There was this fantastic small piano that was suitable for a child just starting to learn the instrument. It was a little worn but in reasonable condition. It was priced at £9.99. I noticed many children played on it when they came in with their parents. If only we could get someone to come in who could actually play it. That would create a good impression. Another very interesting donation was a telescope. This was also in good condition and was reasonably priced at £6.99. We needed the right people in to buy these two unusual donations.

Belinda came out then and took over at the till. She asked me to sort through all the CDs in the shop and in the front storeroom because they hadn't been selling well in the last month. She told me that she had studied my Bar Chart figures and noticed they hadn't been selling many later. I was pleased that Belinda mentioned my Bar Charts, which I do every week on Saturday's sales. This was why I had decided to work these figures out and give breakdowns for each category. Recently, women's goods had been selling well as usual. Also Bric-à-brac and books had been doing well. It meant that Belinda and Rita could take action to increase sales of any goods.

When I went through the CDs on the shelves, I could immediately see why they hadn't been doing well. Most of the music was very bland and middle of the road stuff. It needed an injection of better music, pop, rock, soul and RnB music. I then looked through a few boxes of recently donated CDs and took out the best of them. They included music by Led Zeppelin, Radiohead, Bob Dylan, Van Morrison and The Rolling Stones. I then put the shops code on and the price and put them aside. Next, I went out to the CD section and took off the shelves all the bad selling CDs and put them in the Front Storeroom. I then put out all the new CDs on the shelves in place of these old ones. Finally, I marked up these old CDs with a much cheaper price of 20p and put them on display in a container outside the front of the shop.

Afterwards, I had a break. I made Belinda a coffee, Sadie a green tea and some normal black tea for myself. Grace had brought her own drink in, a coke. I spoke to Sadie and Grace about who would take over from Rita.

"I hope it will be Grace," said Sadie.

"And me," I answered.

"Thanks for your support. If I get the job, I won't be too hard on you," replied Grace.

"Can we have longer breaks?" I asked.

"Also can we have more reductions if we buy items from the shop. Half price isn't enough," Sadie said jokingly.

"What! I haven't got the job yet. I think I will keep things as they are for the time being," responded Grace

It was mid-afternoon by then and Sadie went into the shop to put away most of the Christmas things, except for Christmas cards, diaries and calendars. These would be reduced in price in order to sell them quickly.

After Sadie went out into the shop, I spoke to Grace about the impending job interview.

"Send me a text to let me know how your job interview goes."

"All right."

"When will you know if you get the job?"

"Belinda has said she and the area manager will decide immediately after the three job interviews, probably late afternoon."

"That's good news. At least you don't have to wait until after the weekend."

"I think they want to replace Rita immediately."

"If you get it, do you want to go out on Saturday night to have a drink and maybe a meal as a celebration?"

"That will be great. Maybe not quite as bad as our New Year celebrations when you got drunk."

"Yeah, I did have a few too many. I can only usually handle two or three drinks but I had about four pints," I said. "Mind you, it was a great night."

I then went back out into the shop for the last half an hour. I noticed that most of the Christmas items had been taken down but also that someone had bought the small piano. I went over to speak to Belinda.

"Who bought the small piano?"

"A woman bought it for her grand-daughter. She's just started to take lessons."

"That's good. It hadn't been in the shop long."

"Yes, it had only been donated Thursday."

"That's quick work, selling it so quickly."

"We usually sell good quality items like this very quickly."

"We could do with a buyer for that telescope now."

"A few people have looked at it and shown interest in it. We might sell it next week."

Sadie said goodbye to me and Belinda as we spoke. Belinda thanked her for her hard work.

Belinda prepared to shut the shop. She started to bring in all the containers of reduced-price CDs and DVDs we had outside the front of the shop. I then emptied the bin by the till and the other bins in Belinda's office and the kitchen. When I went into the front storeroom, Grace was cleaning up.

Chapter 17

It was the following Saturday, the day after Grace's job interview. She had texted me yesterday evening to tell me the good news that she had got the job. Therefore, I was looking forward to going into the shop to see her.

As I went into the shop, I said good morning to Belinda who was serving a customer. I was the first volunteer in the shop. I had brought in some old newspapers, old copies of the Daily Mail, my favourite newspaper and The Metro. These came in useful for wrapping up fragile items like glasses, plates and ornaments to stop them breaking or chipping. I took these out to the shop and put them by the till.

Belinda told me to empty the clothing bank first and then work on the till. She informed me that Grace was coming in early so she could show her a lot of the duties of an assistant manager.

While I was emptying the clothing bank, I saw Grace going into the shop. I hurriedly finished taking items out of the bank. It wasn't as full as usual, only three full bags. When I had put the three bags in the front storeroom, I went back out into the shop to take over from Belinda.

I was on the till for the rest of the morning. Sadie came in at 11:30 a.m., a little bit late. She had overslept. Belinda told her to stay on the shop floor and help me on the till. While we worked together on the till, we chatted about Grace getting the job.

"I'm glad Grace has got the job," said Sadie.

"And me. I think she'll do a good job. She really believes in charity shops and she loves this place."

"Yes, she's quite experienced. She has worked here for two years."

"I know she's a friend of ours but we will have to get used to her being our boss from now on," I stated.

"I think she should be all right. I don't think she will let this promotion go to her head. I've worked with someone else who was promoted and she changed a lot, she became power hungry and started to bully me and other workers."

"Yes, I don't think Grace will change much. At least I hope not," I said laughing.

Just then a man came to the counter to buy a pair of trousers. He seemed to like Sadie and was flirting with her. He commented on how nice she was. She ignored a lot of this talk and put the item through the till. He went away smiling at Sadie.

"It looks like you have an admirer, Sadie."

"I have seen him before a few times and he always speaks to me."

"Do you like him?"

"Not really. I behave in a friendly way with him but I try not to encourage him."

"I suppose you are an attractive woman so you are probably used to this attention."

"Yes, it can be flattering but sometimes it does get on your nerves."

"Maybe if he was rich and good looking, it wouldn't be so bad for you."

"I never seem to attract the rich and handsome ones, sadly."

"It's strange that this happens to women. I never get any female admirers showing any interest in me. It doesn't seem to work for men."

Suddenly, Belinda came out into the shop to tell me she wanted to speak to me in the front storeroom. She asked Sadie to carry on working on the till for a while and told her she could ring the bell if she needed any assistance.

When Belinda and I reached the front storeroom, Grace was waiting for us. Belinda explained that there would be a few changes when Grace takes over as assistant manager.

"There won't be too many changes but the new area manager wants the shop to open on Sundays," said Belinda.

"Why's that?" I stated.

"It's because all the other charity shops in Marwood open on Sundays except ours. I have resisted this for many years but this new area manager wants to introduce it now. She reckons it's a good time to do it now that Rita has gone."

"I see. It makes sense."

"Now Grace has agreed to work on Sundays, but needs about at least two more volunteers to help her. Can you work on Sundays, Greg?"

"Yes, I suppose I could. The only problem is that I work most of the week as an inspector and I also work on Saturdays here so I won't have too much time off."

"If it gets too much, you could always have Saturday off and we could get other volunteers in or recruit more volunteers."

"What about if I came in on Sundays for 1:00 p.m.? Then I could have a lie-in in the morning and work from 1:00 p.m. to 4:00 p.m. when the shop shuts," I suggested

"That seems a good idea, I could then try to get someone else to do the morning," said Grace.

"Now Grace is also going to do more hours than Rita, about 30 hours. This includes three days in the week of 8 hours and 6 hours on Sunday, the rate for Sundays will be double time for Grace so that should make up her hours," added Belinda.

"I could ask Sadie if she wants to work on Sundays," stated Grace.

"I will take over the till and ask her to come in and see you. Let me know what she decides, if not, I could ask other volunteers in the week," said Belinda.

Belinda went back out into the shop to work on the till. Shortly afterwards, Sadie came in.

"Hi, Sadie, Belinda and I have just told Greg about having to work on Sundays, can you manage an extra day and work on Sundays?"

"Sundays are bad for me because I like to see some friends on that day. We like to visit the city centre to do shopping and hang out," explained Sadie.

"All right. That's fair enough. Greg can do Sunday afternoons but I need another person for the morning. We shall be opening next Sunday in order to give us a bit of time to get organised."

"What about Adam, Sharon and Maxine?" I suggested.

"I will have to go out to speak to Belinda and ask her to contact these other volunteers to see if they come in."

About five minutes later, Belinda came in and went to her office. She began to make calls to the other volunteers. Sadie replaced her on the till.

Grace then spoke to me to ask me to get the large blackboard out and write a message on it for more volunteers. So I wrote the following message:

VOLUNTEERS REQUIRED TO WORK ON WEEKENDS AT THIS SHOP. IF INTERESTED, PLEASE CONTACT THE MANAGERESS IN THE SHOP.

Grace explained to me that the shop would need a couple more volunteers for Saturday and Sunday.

"I think you may have to give up working on Saturdays and work with me on Sundays. It wouldn't be fair to you to work seven days a week without a rest," stated Grace.

"Yes. That would be all right. I could do other things on Saturday. It will be good to work with you on Sundays."

I then went away to put the large blackboard out in front of the shop. Hopefully, there would be some people showing an interest today. I remembered when I first started at the shop, I had seen this notice outside the shop and I had decided to apply for this unpaid job, one Saturday morning. I was given a form to fill in, which I did the next day and I returned it Monday morning. This was when I was out of work. I thought it would be a good way of learning how to work in a shop to help me get a job. Also, I have always been an animal lover so I thought it would be a rewarding job to do as well.

Afterwards, I put some more books out on the book section. Grace spent a lot of time in Belinda's office discussing things. It was then time for my lunch break. I called into a few shops and then went home for a sandwich, some fruit and a yoghurt.

On my return, Grace updated me on what had been decided.

"Hi, Greg, Belinda and I have sorted out the volunteers for the weekends. On Saturdays, Belinda, Adam, Sadie and hopefully, one of the new volunteers will work in the shop. On Sundays, there will be you, Sharon, me and another new volunteer. Hopefully, we can get three or four people to work on these days. These will probably the busiest days of the week so we will need a fair amount of people in. Are you all right with this?"

"Yes. That seems all right. Is Sharon coming in on Sunday morning?"

"Yes. I want her in early, as she is experienced. Then in the afternoon, you and the new volunteer can work here. I will be in all day."

Later on, I put more books out, emptied the bins and tidied up in the front storeroom. Before leaving, I spoke to Grace, when I got her on her own, about the meal out to celebrate her new job as assistant manager. We agreed to meet at an Indian restaurant in Birmingham, later that night at 8 p.m., Grace said she was looking forward to it. I then left the shop for home. Grace stayed on to be shown how to cash up by Belinda.

Chapter 18

The following Sunday afternoon, I made my way to the charity shop. It felt strange to be working on a Sunday. Adam had been persuaded to go in on Saturdays along with Sadie.

Also, a new volunteer, a girl called Alisha, would work on Saturdays. Another Asian girl, Nisha, would be working on Sunday mornings so there should be enough volunteers to cover all the work. I would miss working on Saturdays because it was the main day of the week and so many things happened.

When I got to the shop, Nisha was on the tilt along with Sharon. I said good afternoon to them both. Sharon introduced me to Nisha. She was an 18-year-old student, who was quite slim, had long black hair and brown eyes. She wore blue jeans and a jumper. Nisha seemed nice and friendly.

I then went into the front storeroom to see Grace. She was sorting through some donated bags.

"Hi, Grace, how are things going?"

"Hi, Greg, yes, things are going well so far. The sales have been quite good this morning."

"I notice Belinda has put up a big sign in the window to say the shop would be opening on Sundays."

"That was a good idea. It's attracted a lot of customers in this morning. I think some were curious to see what the shop would be like on Sundays."

"Maybe some heard that you had taken over from Rita and wanted to see how you were doing."

"Yes, I think some have."

"Did you enjoy the meal last Saturday?" I enquired.

"Yes, I did. It was a nice restaurant."

"I like Indian food. Also, it has a wide variety of food for me to eat."

"We can go again another time."

"What do you want me to do, Grace?"

"Belinda has been studying your Bar Charts for the last few weeks and she isn't happy with the low sales of DVDs. Can you sort through some of the recently donated ones and put them out? Also take off any old DVDs that haven't sold. The DVD section needs refreshing."

"All right. I did this recently with the CDs and it led to an increase in sales."

"Yes." Belinda said.

So, I went out to the DVD section and looked through them. There were quite a lot of mediocre ones out there. Some wouldn't sell if you left them out there all year. I brought about forty into the storeroom to put a new reduced-price label on and to put them in a plastic container to put outside the front of the shop later. Then I checked the box of new DVDs and sorted out about thirty really good ones. Some were classic films, such as 'The Searchers', 'Lawrence of Arabia' and 'Oliver'. Others were classic television programmes such as 'The X Files', 'Spooks' and 'Sherlock.' Also there were several BBC wildlife films, such as 'Planet Earth 2', 'The Life of Mammals' and 'Blue Planet 2'. They should sell fairly quickly.

I took out the DVDs from the covers and put them to one side to put in the container that was put by the till. We didn't put the DVDs in the covers in case they were stolen. I then put the empty covers out on display in the DVD section and put the actual DVDs in the container by the till. Finally, I put the old ones outside on a table in front of the shop. These were reduced to 50p.

After I had sorted these DVDs out, Grace asked me to sort through all the books in the back storeroom. There was this large rack that was stuffed with boxes of books. I usually put out books that had recently been donated in bags but I left these books on the racks for Adam to deal with. He had been off work lately with a bad back and hadn't had much time to go through them. Grace wanted to put other items on this rack so she asked me to free up some space.

I spent an hour sorting through some of these boxes. Most of the books were all right, in good condition and could be sold in the shop. However, there were a small number of books that were very old, stained and a bit tatty. I put these in about three strong bags to give to the ragman for recycling. I made a fair bit of space on the racks but there were still plenty more boxes to look through. I told Grace I would need more time to do these, possibly next Sunday.

After doing this job, I went out into the shop to work on the till with Nisha. Sharon had finished working at 3:00 p.m. I firstly checked the sales to see how we were doing. The sales were over £220, which was good for this time. There was another hour left until the shop shut so we could do even better. I looked around the shop. There were a lot of customers in. Many were browsing. One regular female customer, I recognised, came to the till to buy some books.

"How are you finding the shop on Sundays?" I enquired.

"I'm glad it's open on Sundays. I'm not too keen on shopping on Saturdays because it's too busy. I prefer shopping on Sundays."

"I know what you mean, I live in this town and the High Street is usually packed on Saturdays."

"Also, I like charity shops and this is my favourite one in Marwood."

"That's good to hear. What do you like about this shop?"

"It's much bigger and better than the other ones. I also like the buy one and get one free offer for books."

"The book offer is very popular. It means that you can have two paperbacks for £1.25."

"Some of the other charity shops sell their paperback books for £2 each."

"That's far too dear. I mainly deal with the books here. I try to put a fair price on them. I put more on the hardbacks of course."

"You do a good job."

"It's good to have some positive feedback. So you like the volunteers here then?"

"They're not too bad," she said laughing as she took her books away.

I then spoke to Nisha.

"That's good feedback about this shop. I will have to tell Grace later. How are you finding the job, Nisha?"

"I'm enjoying it."

"Do you like animals?

"Yes. I like animals, that's why I became a volunteer here."

"Do you have any pets?"

"Yes. Two cats."

"What other interests do you have?"

"I'm a big sports fan, particularly football."

"Are you! It's good to see so many women interested in sport these days. What other sports do you like?"

"I like cricket and tennis as well. My favourite sport is football though. My two older brothers are big Liverpool fans and I have become a fan of the team as well," replied Nisha.

"Do you not support a local team then?"

"I do like West Bromwich Albion as well because they are my nearest team."

"Do you like to follow the other football leagues in Europe?"

"Not so much because they are not as competitive as the Premier League," replied Nisha.

"I know what you mean. The German, French, Italian and Scottish leagues are usually won by the same teams year after year."

"Yes. At least the Premier League has had five different winners in the last five seasons."

"It's good to have a football fan working here. I like all the other volunteers here but not many like football, or any sport, so I can't talk to them about this subject."

"Most of my female friends are not football fans either."

"That's a pity. You seem quite unconventional. What I like about most of the volunteers working here are that they are different to most of the people I have worked with, they are quite quirky, in fact."

"I like unconventional people too," said Nisha.

"Grace and Sadie are the same, particularly regarding music. Most young people these days only listen to rap, hip hop and grime but Grace and Sadie don't like that type of music. They both prefer pop, rock and some RnB."

"I'm not much of a rap fan either. I do prefer RnB, pop and dance music, I mainly listen to Capitol Radio."

As it was approaching 4:00 p.m., quite a few customers came to the till to pay for their goods, we took about £30 worth of goods in the last few minutes. I then brought in most of the containers and boxes from the front of the shop, along with the table. Grace came out into the shop and then locked the doors to stop more people from coming in. Nisha went off to get ready to go. She then left at just after 4 p.m. I said goodbye to Nisha and told her I would see her next Sunday.

"Nisha's a nice girl. She's worked hard on the till."

"That's good to hear. Sometimes, we get lucky with these volunteers."

"I think she should fit in well here."

"That's good. We have done well for the first Sunday. The sales are £280.50," said Grace looking at the figures on the till.

"That's very good," I replied.

"That's more than the sales for yesterday."

"Belinda won't be too pleased," I said laughing,

"I suppose there will be times when she does better than me. We can't get too competitive."

"Can I still have the sales figures for today so I can continue working out the Bar Charts?"

"Yes. I will print a copy for you now."

After looking at the figures, I said that women's sales had done well again but men's sales were well down."

"We seem to be struggling to get enough good quality men's clothes at the moment," stated Grace.

"I work with someone who wants to get rid of some of his clothes," I said.

After about fifteen minutes, Grace came over with a navy handbag. She looked pleased.

"It was still here so I grabbed it before anyone else."

"How much is it?"

"£4.99. It's a real bargain," said Grace.

"All right, let's go and pay for it."

"Where to, next?" I enquired.

"Mind. It's on this side of the road."

'Mind' charity shop was fairly similar to Barnado's. It wasn't big enough for all the goods there. It was too cramped. However, there was some good quality items there. They had some excellent calendars and greetings cards. Grace was particularly interested in the calendars.

"I need a calendar and I noticed some good ones here the other day," said Grace.

"They do look good. I like the animal one, which has animals painted by an artist."

"Yes. That's good. I also like the calendar of places in Britain, such as Stratford, Windsor and Brighton."

"Take your time. I will go off and look at the book section," I stated.

I wasn't too impressed with the books. They didn't have much stock and they were quite dear, two for £3. Nearby, the DVDs and CDs were marked up at a similar price The Bric-à-brac section was good though, containing lots of unusual ornaments. Shortly after, Grace came back with the animal calendar. She told me she liked how artistic it was and that it would look good on her wall. It cost £3.99, which I paid for at the till.

"That's two down, five to go," said Grace,

"That's a nice calendar. I might buy one myself another time. It's not too bad in there, is it?"

"Yes, there's some good stuff in there."

"Where to, next?" I enquired.

"Let's cross the road and try 'Age UK'."

"What are you looking for there?"

"I saw some good clothes in their earlier in the week."

"All right, I will have a browse around the shop while you look at the women's section."

I slowly made my way around the shop, looking at the books, DVDs, CDs and men's clothes. There was a reasonable choice of these goods but I wasn't tempted to buy anything. Grace came up to me after a while with two tops.

"I can't decide which of these to buy. I would like them both."

"How much are they?"

"They are £2.50 each."

"If you can't choose one, I suppose you could have both and miss out on going to one of the other shops."

"Would that be all right?"

"Yes. If that's what you want."

"OK. I will miss out on going to Oxfam. Let's go to 'British Heart Foundation' next," said Grace.

"All right."

This charity shop had probably got the best window display in Marwood. One of the volunteers must have had plenty of experience of doing these displays. They looked so good. On one side of the window were clothes artistically exhibited on mannequins and on the other side of the window were displays of books. Most of the people I knew were impressed by this window display. However, inside the shop, it was not as impressive, their books were over-priced. Some paperbacks were £2. Others were £1. I didn't understand why.

"You have spent just under £14 so you haven't got much money left," I stated.

"Yes. I have to be careful. When I was here the other day, I did see a nice ornament of a dog. I will try to get it."

"OK. I will have a look around."

While I was in the book section, a volunteer put some books out. I then spoke to him. "Why have you got some paperback books priced at £1 and some priced at £2?"

"We have been told to charge more for newer books," said the man.

"I see but other shops don't do this."

"I know, but our manager wants to do it like this."

Grace then returned with her ornament of a dog.

"I see you have got your dog."

"I'm glad. I was worried it would be sold."

"It looks nice. How much is it?"

"£1.99."

"Let's go to pay for it."

"That's nearly £16," I said.

"I know. I haven't got much left now."

"Where to, next?"

"Acorns, it's just up the road."

"So, is this the last one today?"

"Yes. I'll leave our shop until tomorrow, Sunday. I can have a good look around without anyone noticing."

We entered Acorns. It was the cleanest and tidiest of all the charity shops we had visited. It was a similar size to the other shops but as they had less stock than the others, it meant that the goods weren't squeezed into a small space. It was laid out well. There were a lot of customers there.

"What are you looking for here?" I asked.

"I would like a birthday card. It's my best friend, Emma's birthday in early February."

I looked at the birthday cards along with Grace. They were good quality ones. They had humorous ones, ones with ages on, some for men and some for women. Grace chose a humorous animal card. It was of a group of penguins huddled together in the cold. The caption read: What friends are for. Our heating bills should be a lot less now.

"That's a funny birthday card," I said.

"Yes. She's an animal lover like me but she does have a good sense of humour."

"I haven't met her yet. What's she like?"

"She is fairly similar to me in personality but in appearance, she is different. She is a brunette and she's taller than me."

"Right. How much is the card?"

"£1.99."

"I'll pay for it now."

"Shall we have a break and go for a drink at the coffee shop? We can have a chat about the morning," suggested Grace.

"OK. As long as you're paying. I'm skint. I've just spent nearly £20," I said jokingly.

"All right. I'll pay."

We went to the local café. I had a cup of tea and Grace had a coke.

"Did you enjoy your charity shop shopping spree?"

"It was very enjoyable. I have often wanted to do that and I also learnt a fair bit about our competitors."

"What did you learn?"

"That all the charity shops in Marwood have their good points but many lack our space."

"Yes. I think that's our biggest advantage over the other shops," I stated.

"Another thing our shop does better is we recycle more and we have a clothing and shoe bank."

"That's right. No other charity shop has one in this town."

"The only thing I saw that I would like to introduce into our shop are greetings cards, I might try to get some in our shop. I might suggest this to Belinda."

"Are you that interested in selling them in the shop?"

"Yes. I think they could be a good way of making money and they would add variety to the stock. I might make some enquiries at a few card shops to see if some could donate old stock to us," replied Grace.

"That sounds like a good idea, it's worth trying."

"I will speak to Belinda about it when I see her next."

"Are there any other changes you would like to make?"

"We need better volunteers. The ones in the other charity shops seem better than ours," said Grace.

"What!" I gasped.

"I'm only joking. Seriously, I was thinking about the shop's strengths and weaknesses. The strengths are its size, it's excellent women's clothes section, its good recycling facilities, its buy one get one free offers and its volunteers, who are all hard working and reliable," stated Grace.

"What do you think about the shops weak points?" I asked.

"I think, its location and its poor window display. We can't do much about where the shop is situated but we can improve the window display."

"Yes. It's a pity the shop is not nearer to the main shops in the town, such as Aldi and Poundland. We are a bit isolated from these shops so our customers have to make more of an effort to come up to the top of the high street."

"I will speak to Belinda about improving the window display. I could get Sharon to do it on Sunday. She's experienced at doing these types of things."

"OK. Let's forget about work now. What are you doing for your birthday?"

"I'm going out with my best friend, Emma, on Tuesday night."

"What about us going somewhere next weekend?"

"All right. What about next Sunday after work?" asked Grace.

"Yes. That should be all right."

"We could relax and have a drink. What are you doing now?" asked Grace.

"I'm going into Birmingham to buy you a surprise birthday present."

"Oh good. Any clues?"

"It's such a surprise that even I don't know what to buy you yet. I will give it some thought. I can give it to you at the shop tomorrow."

"Thanks. See you tomorrow."

I kissed her on the cheek and we parted. Grace took all her charity shop presents home and I set off for Birmingham.

Chapter 20

It was the Sunday after Grace's birthday and I made my way to the shop. The weather had turned bad overnight and was snowing heavily. I just hoped this snow didn't deter our customers from coming to the shop. We had done well for the first two Sundays, reaching nearly £300 on sales. Grace was pleased with these sales. Also the sales on Saturday had remained steady. Thankfully, we weren't taking business from Belinda.

When I reached the shop, I noticed Sharon was in the front window moving things around. It looked like she was trying to refresh the window display.

I said good afternoon to Nisha and went into the front storeroom. Grace was there steaming some dresses.

"Hi, Grace, it's snowing heavily now," I said as I shook the snow from my coat.

"Hi, Greg. How deep is it?"

"Not too deep yet."

"I just hope it doesn't snow for too long. I don't want to shut the shop early."

"I'll keep an eye on it. How did your birthday go on Tuesday?"

"It went well. My friend, Emma, bought me some nice presents, perfume and a wildlife DVD I wanted. We went out for a drink on Tuesday night."

"Did you have some nice presents from your family?"

"Yes. My mom and dad gave me some money and my sister bought me a book I wanted."

"What was the book about?"

"It's called, '*How to understand Men*'," Grace said with a straight face.

"I think you are having me on, aren't you? How did you like my surprise present?"

"It was lovely. Thanks. I like Thorntons chocolate. The message you had put on was very good: 'Happy Birthday, assistant manager at the RSPCA.' Nice touch."

"I thought you'd like it. Have you chosen your birthday present from this shop yet?" I asked Grace.

"I had a quick look around when I arrived. There's a couple of paperback books I would like. I have put them aside to pay for them later."

"Don't forget you have both the buy one get one free offer and the half price charge because you work here."

"That's right. I will only need to pay 62p instead of £1.25," said Grace.

"In total, you will have spent £18.58," I stated after working it out on a piece of paper.

"So, I have saved you nearly £1.50."

"It's amazing how many items you can buy in charity shops for less than £20."

"I bought 7 items. The handbag, the calendar, two tops, an ornament of a dog, a birthday card and two books. That's good value for money."

"I'm pleased you like all these goods. What do you want me to do today?" I replied.

"Can you work on the till for a while? Also, can you ask Sharon to come in here to help me sort through these donations when she has finished improving the window display and had her break?"

"All right."

I then went out into the shop to see Sharon. When I reached the front of the shop, I could see how much better the front window looked. On one side of the window, she had put three large mannequins and on them, she had displayed three winter coats, all high quality and almost brand-new. On the other side of the window, she had put one book rack to show some books along with a big sign informing the customers about the buy one get one free offer. Also, there was a shoe rack showing high quality women's shoes which looked brand-new on top of their original boxes. Some women donated new shoes without them even wearing them. It was an impressive display.

Sharon was finishing off the window display so I went up to speak to her. "Hi, Sharon, how's it going?"

"Hi, Greg, it's been good. I have just got it how I want it."

"You've done a good job. It looks impressive."

"Thanks. I've done plenty of these before. I enjoy doing them."

"Grace will be pleased."

"I hope she likes it. Hopefully, it will help to encourage more customers in," added Sharon,

"Grace told me to tell you that can you help her sorting bags of donations after your break."

"All right. I could do with a drink and a sit down."

"See you later," I said.

I then went over to talk to Nisha, who was working on the till.

"Hi, Nisha, how are you?"

"Not too bad, thanks."

"How has it been today?"

"It's been reasonably busy. We are doing well on sales again. It was nearly £200 when I last looked half an hour ago."

"That's good. We have done very well so far on the two previous Sunday's. What time are you finishing today?"

"I'm going at 2:00 p.m. when Sharon has finished her break."

"All right."

"I might have to go earlier on some Sundays when Liverpool is playing on this day."

"Oh, yes, you're a Liverpool fan, aren't you?

"I am. I never miss a game."

"They are doing well at the moment so I can understand you not wanting to miss any games."

Just then I heard a loud crash in the back of the shop, a customer had dropped an ornament. This sometimes happened. I went over to investigate. A man had dropped a ship in a bottle and it had broken. He looked worried.

"Oh, no! I spent ages putting that ship in the bottle," I said trying not to laugh.

"I'm sorry it slipped out of my hand," said the man.

"Don't worry, I was only joking. This usually happens a few times a month but we don't make too much of a fuss about it."

"Thanks."

"Accidents can happen. I will get a dustpan and brush to clean it up."

About ten minutes later, this man came to the till to buy a shirt and a DVD. I didn't know if he felt guilty about breaking the ornament or he would have bought them anyway.

When it was quiet, I looked outside the shop to check on the snow. It had stopped snowing. Thankfully, it wasn't too deep. It had gone colder though so I went back inside.

A little later, another customer caused me a slight problem. I had gone into the kitchen to make everyone a drink and had just finished when Nisha rang the bell to get me to come out and help her. I gave everyone their drinks and then went out to the shop to speak to Nisha.

"Greg, there's a man over there who is acting suspiciously. He's wearing dark glasses and it looks like he is pretending to be blind."

"All right, I will go and see if I can help him."

When I went over to him, he was straining his eyes to look at the size of a pair of socks.

"Do you need any help?" I asked.

"Yes. Can you tell me what size these socks are?"

"They are 6-11. What size are you?"

"I'm size 9."

"I'm the same size. These should fit you."

"They are £2.99. Can you give me a reduction? I'm disabled," said the man.

"I can't really because they are good quality wool socks and they are brand-new and still in the pack."

"Are you sure?"

"These socks would probably cost about £8 in a shop."

"Oh, all right. Let's see how much money I have left. I need some money for my bus fare. I have enough. I'll buy them."

After he had paid for them, I told Nisha that I thought he was genuinely partially sighted but he was trying it on with us.

"I thought there was something fishy about him," stated Nisha.

"I think he was trying to take advantage of us because he is disabled. I can help him to a certain extent but I can't give price reductions on cheap items like those. If the item was expensive, I could call Grace out to knock a few pounds off."

At 2:00 p.m., Sharon finished her break and went to help Grace sort through lots of donated bags of mainly clothes. A lot of bags had been donated yesterday and it was taking a long time to get through them. Grace needed some help. Nisha went home and I continued on the till until the shop shut. Sales were gradually going up during the afternoon.

I looked around the shop, there were quite a lot of customers in browsing. Then two customers bought two high-priced items. One man bought a £15 jacket. This was priced high because of the brand and because it was in very good condition. It looked like it had hardly been worn. Another customer, a young woman, bought a coat for £20, again a high-quality, branded coat. Sales were brisk. With half an hour to go, we had taken over £270.

Then Rita and her daughter's friendly dog, Jack, called into the shop unexpectedly.

"Hi, Rita. It's good to see you. How are you?"

"Not too bad, thanks."

"How's your husband?"

"He's had his operation and is recovering well. He can't get around much though. I'm having to do a lot for him."

"That's good."

"How are your sales for Sunday?" asked Rita.

"Very good. We are making over £270 most Sundays. Grace is very pleased with them."

"That's great news."

"Do you miss it here?" I said as I stroked Jack, her lovable dog.

"I miss Belinda, the volunteers and some of the customers but not the work. I have lost interest in it now. It has become too tiring for me."

"I understand. You have worked here for a long time."

"Yes. Ten years is long enough."

"Do you want to speak to Grace? She's in the front store room sorting through plenty of donated bags."

"Don't mention sorting through bags. I have looked through about a million of them in my time," replied Rita laughing as she went away to speak to Grace.

It was nearly time to shut the shop so I brought in all the containers of DVDs, CDs and records that were outside on the bargain table. Shortly after, Rita and her dog, Jack, came out to leave. She said she would call in occasionally to see us. The last few customers along with Sharon left the shop and I locked the door. Grace came out then to check the sales figures for the day.

"Great! We've gone over £300."

"That's good news. It was over £270 when I last looked. We sold a lot of good quality items in the last half an hour."

"It was good to see Rita again earlier, wasn't it?" said Grace.

"I was pleased to see her again. Won't she miss the money?" I said.

"Not really. Her husband had a very well-paid job before he retired and he has a good pension. They are fairly rich."

"All right. Let's cash up and then go for that drink."

"OK, the first rounds on you," replied Grace.

When Grace and I reached the local pub, we were glad to see that it wasn't too packed. There had been a live football game on earlier but it had finished and the football supporters had left. I fetched Grace a coke and I had a lager.

"It's great to be able to relax after a hard day at the shop," I stated.

"What do you mean, you only did half a day?"

"I will rephrase that. It's great to be able to relax after a hard half a day at the shop."

"That's more like it, part-timer," said Grace laughing.

"All right. I will admit you worked harder than me," I said grudgingly.

"I feel tired. I'm glad I did so many bags. There won't be so many for the volunteers to do on Monday."

"Things are going well for you on Sundays."

"Yes. I was worried about working on Sundays in case we didn't attract enough customers. We are doing well so far."

"Maybe our customers have always wanted the shop to be open on Sundays but went to somewhere else as we weren't open."

"Maybe," said Grace, sipping on her coke.

"It's amazing how things have changed for us for the better in the last few months," I stated.

"Yes. I've got this new job and I'm seeing you."

"Have you ever got the feeling that things have improved for both of us because of the shop?"

"What do you mean?"

"Well, before I worked at the shop, I had lost my job and my house and I was struggling on zero-hour contract jobs with little work. Now, I have a steadier job and I'm seeing you."

"I see what you mean. Do you think it's because of the shop?"

"I think so. I have always found it therapeutic to work at the shop. It has helped get me through some very tough times. I think the shop has something to do with it," I explained.

Suddenly, we both noticed Shelley had come into the pub with a friend. She hadn't seen us. I went over to speak to her.

"Hi, Shelley, how are you. I haven't seen you for a while."

"Oh, hi, Greg. It's good to see you. I'm fine. How are you?"

"I'm not too bad. I'm having a drink with Grace. We have just finished working at the shop."

"I've heard you work on Sundays now. Can I come over to speak to you both?"

"Yeah sure."

Shelley asked her friend to wait for her for a short while. Then we both went over to speak to Grace.

"Hi, Shelley. Good to see you."

"Hi, Grace. I hear you're the new assistant manager."

"Yes, I have recently taken on the job."

"Are you enjoying it?"

"Definitely. It's my dream job," replied Grace.

"How is your job, Shelley?" I asked.

"I have a new job now. My old job wasn't too good. I didn't get on with some of the people at the shop so I have changed my job. I work in a factory now, which means that I can work on Saturdays and Sundays."

"If you want, you could come back to work at the shop. We could do with good, experienced volunteers," said Grace.

"Do you mean that? I've missed working at the shop," replied Shelley.

"What day can you work?"

"Can I work on Sundays? I get on well with you and Greg."

"All right. I will speak to Sharon to see if she wants a few Sundays off. She told me yesterday that she wanted to go out with her daughter to a few places. I can get her to have the next few Sundays off. Also, Nisha can have the occasional Sunday off. Can you work next Sunday at 10:00 a.m.?"

"That would be great," replied Shelley.

"Hey, this means the old team will be back in business at the shop. Grace, Shelley and Greg. It will be just like the old days," I stated.

"Maybe you are right about the shop, Greg," said Grace.